Title Page
The Graham Files: Shattered Mandates
A Novel by
Eric Glenn
Graham Legacy Publishing™
Charlotte, North Carolina
2025

Copyright Page
© 2025 Eric Glenn
 Published by Graham Legacy Publishing™
Mint Hill, North Carolina
Printed in the United States of America
Dedication Page

Dedication
To my grandchildren—
Anthony Glenn, Eric J. Glenn, William Glenn, Brooklynn "Pie" Glenn, and Solaya Mills—
May your names echo with pride, your roots run deep like ancient trees, and your minds blaze brighter than the stars we were never meant to reach. This book is not just a story— it is a torch, lit by the hands of those who came before.
Carry it forward.
Light the path.
Change the world.

Epigraph

"They banned books.
So we memorized them.
They defunded schools.
So we opened sanctuaries.
They called us extremists.
So we called roll."

— The Graham Files: Shattered Mandates

Prologue: The Fire Next Time

They never expected the students to fight back.
Not like this.
Not with Molotov Cocktails or protest signs. But with archived syllabi printed on mimeograph machines, tucked into the spines of library discards. With radical footnotes hidden in footnotes. With codeswitches turned into actual code.
They banned books.
So, we memorized them.
They defunded schools.
So, we opened sanctuaries.
They called us extremists.
So, we called roll.
The fire didn't come in riots. It came in ripples—each whisper a spark. Each journal entry, each underground lecture, each reclaimed textbook a torch passed hand-to-hand beneath the notice of those too powerful to imagine being powerless.
ScholarForge wasn't a school anymore.
It was a diaspora.
An insurgency of intellect.
A long memory sharpened into doctrine.
And like all fires that start underground—
it was spreading.

Table of Contents

Part I: Codes and Crimes

Part II: Resistance and Recall

Chapter 1: Doctrine of Dust

The classroom wasn't marked.
No bell. No cameras. No pledge recited.
Just peeling linoleum, six salvaged desks,
and a chalkboard dug out of an abandoned
magnet school.
Perfect cover.
Langston Graham stood at the front of the
room, sleeves rolled back, his breath
visible in the cold. Outside, a city groaned
under the weight of denial. Inside, the
truth warmed the walls like a furnace. Ten
students—some his former scholars,
others exiles from shuttered schools—sat
in silence. They were not here for credits.
They were here for weaponry. Cognitive
arms. Ancestral algorithms. Langston
placed a weathered pamphlet on the desk.
"Mandate for Equity in Higher Education,
1971," he said. "Commissioned. Redacted.
Buried." He paused.
"Anyone know why?"
A hand shot up—Zora Patel, seventeen,
expelled from two districts for "disruptive
political engagement."
"Because it said education wasn't
enough without redistribution of access,"
she replied. "Because it proved the
system's real priority was containment,
not enlightenment." Langston nodded.
"Correct," he said. "And for that, it was
marked for deletion."
The students leaned in.
"This," he continued, tapping the paper,
"is what I call the Doctrine of Dust. The
process of burying truth beneath neglect.

Not destruction—just denial. And yet…"
He stepped back and lifted the chalk, scrawling across the board in broad strokes:
ScholarForge: Phase II
Below it: Syllabus. Subversion. Sanctuary.
The students scribbled furiously. But Jamal Baker, Marcus's younger cousin, glanced up.
"What if they shut this place down too?"
Langston met his eyes. Didn't blink.
"They will." Silence.
"But the point of fire," he added softly, "isn't to avoid the burn. It's to forge the future."
He clicked the projector remote.
The screen lit with grayscale footage:
Police raids on literacy circles.
Empty libraries turned drone-hubs.
News tickers framing ScholarForge as a "subversive radical learning cell."
Langston let the silence stretch. "They call it sedition," he said. "We call it syllabus."
Footsteps echoed in the hallway— measured, familiar. A coded knock tapped the rhythm of an old gospel refrain: We've come this far by faith. The side door opened.
Dr. Ysabel Rojas stepped inside. Wrapped in a thick wool coat, her gray streaked braids pulled back, she moved with quiet precision. A former tenured historian exiled from her post at Columbia after defending student-led curriculum strikes, she was now chief architect of ScholarForge's new pedagogy division.
She gave Langston a small nod. "They're

ready. The Eastern Corridor just lit green."
Langston turned back to the students.
"This is our final session in this building,"
he said. "But it's not graduation. It's
deployment."
He opened a small wooden case. Inside,
ten brass keys. Each engraved with a
number and a sigil. "These keys open our
safehouses— bookshelves behind
barbershops, church closets repurposed
into media servers, forgotten storage units
reimagined as memory vaults. Inside:
encrypted texts. Banned literature.
Oracles. Oral traditions transcribed and
archived." One by one, he handed the keys
out. "When you walk out that door, you're
not just students. You're custodians of the
rebellion."
Langston turned back to the chalkboard.
He erased Phase II and replaced it
with: Shattered Mandates He circled
the phrase twice. "When an empire
breaks its own promises," he said, "we
don't gather the pieces to mourn them.
We gather them to sharpen them."
He set the chalk down.
Outside, the wind kicked dust against the
windows.
Inside, memory stirred—no longer content
to survive. It had come to confront.

Chapter 2: Wellspring Protocol

Langston stood beneath the old laundromat in East Newark, where the false floor beneath dryer #3 led to a stairwell so narrow it felt like falling into the throat of the past.
The basement smelled of rust, sage, and ink.
Flickering LEDs revealed a tight room no larger than a studio apartment, walls lined with encrypted servers disguised as vintage stereo cabinets, and three folding tables stacked with aged schoolbooks, barcode-free.
On one of the tables sat a cracked copy of Up From Slavery, a flash drive glued inside the back cover. Another book, The Wretched of the Earth, had been rebound as Advanced Algebra II.
Langston ran his hand along a reinforced crate stamped with an old shipping manifest: WELLSPRING PROTOCOL BETA UNIT 3 — NOT FOR PUBLIC USE.
Beside it stood a man with dark eyes and a shaved head, wearing a workman's uniform that read "Franklin HVAC." No one called him by his real name anymore.
"Everything's clean," he said. "Nodes alpha through gamma are mirrored. Access remains dark unless pinged with verse."
Langston raised an eyebrow. "Which verse?"

The man grinned. "Micah 6:8. Old school." Langston smiled faintly. "Do justly. Love mercy. Walk humbly."

The unit clicked open. Inside: six hand sized drives, each protected by a temperature-controlled shell, and two dozen printed curriculum packets disguised as church bulletins. Everything ScholarForge needed to seed the next wave of resistance.

Langston nodded.

"Send two to Chicago," he said. "One to Savannah. One to the old St. Judah Baptist Church in the Bronx. And keep the last two mobile. Shadow routes only." The man paused. "And the archive protocols?"

Langston took a deep breath.

"We activate the secondary memory wells next week. First through elder libraries. Then the transit stops. The school bus radios are ready?"

He nodded. "Our drivers are solid. Trained by Miss Elsie. They know the drops, and the sermons to use if they're stopped."

Langston folded his arms, looking around the bunker.

The revolution hadn't gone silent. It had gone multilingual. Each node— each hidden archive, encrypted playlist, textbook remixed and released under Creative Commons—was now part of a mosaic too sprawling to track. He turned to the HVAC man one last time. "Frank," Langston said, "when they try to erase us again, what will they find?" Frank reached behind a shelf and pulled out a cracked composition book.

Inside it was a child's scrawl:
"You can't kill what remembers you."

Chapter 3: The Norrington Doctrine

The broadcast wasn't flashy. Just a navy-blue curtain, an American flag, and Charles Norrington seated behind a walnut desk.
It was framed like a presidential fireside chat. Calm. Assured. Dangerous.
"America has always defended free speech," Norrington began, his voice dipped in the honey of reason, "but sedition masquerading as education must be confronted."
Behind him, graphics faded in a montage of grainy ScholarForge activity—anonymous faces in lecture rooms, chalkboards with banned texts, fragments of encrypted student essays.
The chyron below read:
"Hidden Curriculum or Hidden Conspiracy?"
Langston watched from the safehouse, jaw tight.
Norrington went on. "In recent months, we've identified multiple rogue educators leveraging shadow learning networks to undermine social cohesion and national unity. These are not teachers. These are insurgents." He folded his hands, the ring on his finger catching the light: a silver eagle gripping a key.
"Effective immediately, my office is launching a bipartisan national inquiry into subversive educational syndicates. We call this initiative... The Norrington Doctrine."
Langston didn't laugh.

He'd expected this.
They always name the knife before they stab with it.
The Doctrine gave federal agencies a blank check—surveillance without warrants, raids without warning, legal reclassifications of learning hubs as "unregulated ideological training grounds."
In the corner of the screen, a reporter's voice piped in:
"One group under scrutiny is ScholarForge, which authorities say may be linked to data laundering and intellectual radicalization across multiple states. The group has not responded to official inquiries." Langston
clicked off the feed. The Doctrine wasn't just about crushing ScholarForge.
It was about rewriting the definition of rebellion.
And then criminalizing it.

ScholarForge Insert – The Brass That Binds
Recovered Log Entry | Internal Memo: ScholarForge Archives | Sector 7 – Dupont Quadrant

"We don't wear uniforms. We wear memory.
We don't shout resistance. We whisper truth through action."

— Founder's Ledger, Vol. I, Dr. Langston

Elkanah Graham

This field account, corroborated by Marcus Elijah Baker, was archived following an incident in Northwest D.C. The subject—codename *Torchbearer Primus*—was identified by his reversible brass insignia and safely extracted to a secure ScholarForge enclave. The presence of Monroe confirms high-value protocol clearance. Memory affirmed. Operation sealed.

Insert: The Brass That Binds

The air on the corner of 14th and G Street NW was thick with humidity and tension. Summer in the capital had a way of clinging to everything—clothing, concrete, and conflict.

Marcus Baker had been walking briskly from an early meeting with an education equity group when the scene caught his attention. Two officers stood over a young man, no older than seventeen, who was seated on the curb with his palms up and fingers splayed. A third officer stood back, arms folded, staring like a hawk measuring a mouse.

The student was well-dressed—navy blazer, khakis, oxford shoes still dusted from walking. His messenger bag lay on its side, contents scattered. Books on policy, history, and philosophy littered the sidewalk like fallen relics.

Marcus's first instinct was to keep moving. This wasn't his fight. Not today. But something nagged at him.

Then he saw it.

On the inside of the student's blazer—visible only because the police had forced him to open it—was a plain brass pin affixed to the lining. To the untrained eye, it looked like a discarded button. But Marcus had seen the reverse once before, inside Dr. Graham's study. He knew what it was.
ScholarForge.

Subtle. Timeless. A miniature anvil with a torch and an open book atop it. The forge of minds. A symbol that bore no recognition to the average person, but that lit a fire in those who knew.

Marcus pulled back, retreating behind a nearby parked food truck. He fished out his phone and didn't bother texting.

"Monroe," he said low into the receiver. "Langston's not gonna believe this. I just saw a ScholarForge kid being hassled by D.C. Metro. He's got the pin."

There was no hesitation. "Where?" she asked.

"Fourteenth and G. Near the Dupont side. Light brown skin, tight fade, gold-rim glasses. The kind of kid who'd quote Du Bois before breakfast."

Monroe's response was clipped. "I'm coming."

Seven minutes later, the deep growl of Langston's Benz cut through the ambient traffic. Monroe stepped out, hair wrapped in a navy scarf, sunglasses perched high. She wore a linen blouse and slate-gray slacks—simple, but commanding. She moved with the energy of someone who answered to no one except her own mission.
"Officers," she called as she approached, voice crisp, accent faintly British. "Is there a problem here?"

The lead officer turned toward her, cautious. "Ma'am, we've received a report about a suspicious individual loitering. We're asking questions."

Monroe arched a brow and produced a slim leather folio. "This individual is a student under private tutelage, enrolled in an advanced academic initiative with federal documentation. I'd be happy to call Director Hanley in the Inspector General's office, if you'd like to explain the disruption of a sanctioned educational program."
The cop blinked. "That won't be necessary."

She turned to the student, extending a hand. "Let's get you out of the sun."

The student stood shakily, but when Monroe gently reached forward and adjusted his lapel, revealing the brass pin and exposing the ScholarForge emblem within, she whispered, "You did well. You wore it with dignity."

Without another word, she guided him into the back seat of the Benz. The car pulled away, smooth and deliberate.

Marcus remained on the sidewalk, invisible to the officers and passersby. He felt the weight of the moment settle on him like an invisible cloak. He had seen behind the veil.

That wasn't just a student. That was a flamebearer.

And ScholarForge wasn't a metaphor.

It was a movement.

Chapter 4: Memory Crimes Unit

Agent Charlene Wexler didn't care for children.

But she did love a clean sweep.

She stood outside the Booker T. Washington Community Center in Birmingham, Alabama, zipping up a Kevlar vest labeled MCU — Memory Crimes Unit.

Behind her, a team of twelve agents filed out of unmarked vans. Drones buzzed overhead. A warrant blinked on her tablet: Approved — Memory Violation Class A: Unauthorized Instruction, Restricted Material Possession.

Inside, Ms. Odessa Fields was teaching her Saturday class—ages 8 to 13—how to cross-reference oral history with public transit records from the 1960s Freedom Rides.

The lesson plan was flagged last week.

Too accurate.

Too Black.

Too brave.

Wexler gave the signal.

Doors crashed open.

Children screamed. Papers scattered. A recording device disguised as a toy truck was seized, its memory drive yanked and sealed.

Ms. Fields stepped forward, hands raised but eyes burning.

"I'm not hiding anything." Wexler's voice was cold steel. "You already did." She turned to one of her sub-agents. "Strip the walls. Confiscate all analog texts. Check the floorboards for caches."

Downstairs, behind a filing cabinet, they found it: a faded copy of The Miseducation of the Negro with margin notes in Swahili and Gullah. Wexler snapped on gloves and held it like it was plutonium.

"You see," she whispered, "the real threat isn't rebellion. It's memory."

Chapter 5: Mandates from Above

The Graham Files: Shattered Mandates
Langston sat motionless, the glow of three encrypted news feeds flickering across his lined face.
A man stood behind a presidential seal, wrapped in flags and flanked by teleprompters. His tone was polished, his smile practiced. His speech bore the title: "American Priorities — Safety. Values. Power."
Langston leaned forward. He had heard these words before. Not from a man in a suit, but from men in uniforms. From governors. From secretaries of education and homeland security. The names changed. The strategy didn't.
"We will restore order at our borders. No more catch-and-release. No more sanctuary. No more open gates to chaos."
The crowd applauded.
Langston did not.
His mind drifted to the Haitian refugees in the 1980s, turned back at sea. To the 1917 Immigration Act, which limited the entry of Caribbean and African peoples under a veil of national security. To the Black asylum seekers labeled as threats, denied entry for having the wrong skin tone, the wrong passport, or the wrong prayers.
"This ain't new," he muttered. Beside him, Dr. Ysabel Rojas scrolled through the policy outline on a cracked tablet.
IMMIGRATION & BORDER POLICY
End humanitarian parole.

Reinstate "Remain in Mexico." Expand military presence at border zones.

Designate cartels as foreign terrorist organizations.

"It's the Fugitive Slave Act for the modern age," Langston said, eyes fixed. "Except now, they're framing escape as invasion."

Rojas didn't look up. "Black migrants will suffer first. And worst."

Next came the domestic economic planks.

ENERGY & ECONOMY: MAKE AMERICA AFFORDABLE

Deregulate fossil fuel industries. End renewable energy subsidies.

Withdraw from international climate coalitions.

Langston sighed. "More smokestacks in our zip codes. Just like St. James Parish. Just like Cancer Alley."

He remembered his grandfather's lungs—the way they rattled each winter from the chemical air drifting over the bayou. "This isn't affordability," he said. "It's extraction. Again."

Rojas tapped the final tab.

GOVERNMENT REFORM: CUTTING THE FAT

Freeze federal hiring in 'non-essential' sectors.

Eliminate DEI initiatives.

Mandate return to on-site work for federal employees.

Langston chuckled bitterly. "Whenever Black folks gain ground, they change the definition of essential." He remembered reading about the postal strikes of the 1970s—how Black workers demanded dignity and were met with tear gas and threats of federal intervention. Langston had been too young to witness it firsthand, but the stories were etched into the margins of his grandfather's Bible and the footnotes of books rarely found in school libraries.

He remembered how every gains program—affirmative action, federal internships, public sector training—had been targeted with surgical precision.

"DEI was a flashlight," he said. "Dim, but better than nothing. Now they want darkness."

The last section chilled him most.

SOCIAL VALUES: BRING BACK TRADITION

Legally restore binary gender definitions. Rename "problematic" landmarks. Punish schools that "undermine American heritage."

Langston stared at the screen. "Same playbook they used in the Lost Cause," he said. "Rename. Reframe. Replace."

He thought of how they'd torn down Reconstruction history and replaced it with Confederate statues. How they'd gutted Black-led schools after Brown v. Board, then blamed integration for the loss. How "tradition" always meant a return to someone else's comfort—and Black erasure.

Rojas looked up. "They're not just writing policy. They're writing permission."

Langston nodded.

"And permission turns into mandates.
Mandates for forgetting." He crossed
the room to his journal and opened to a
blank page.
Across the top he wrote:
Operating Thesis #2 — Shattered
Mandates
"When memory becomes a threat, policy
becomes a weapon."
He turned toward the back wall—where
the plans for ScholarForge Phase III were
tacked in layers. Mobile classrooms.
Covert server banks. Multilingual
broadcast stations hidden in low-frequency
radio networks.
The underground was awake.
But this was no longer about secrecy.
Langston stood, voice low but certain.
"They've named their mandates. Now it's
time we name ours."

Chapter 6: The First Raid

The Graham Files: Shattered Mandates
The old church basement on 133rd and Lenox didn't look like much from the outside.
The front doors were warped from the weather. The neon sign that once read ST. ELIJAH BAPTIST MISSION had been half burned out for years—now it just hummed: ST. I—BAPT—MISS—. No one noticed it anymore. That was the point.
But beneath its cracked foundation, ScholarForge Node 12 pulsed quietly. Inside, ten middle school students were seated in mismatched chairs, deep in a lesson on redlined neighborhoods and the buried truths of urban renewal. A former city planner turned ScholarForge educator—Ms. Hollis—projected maps onto the stone wall using a salvaged smartboard.
"This used to be the Third Ward," she explained. "Now they call it Heritage Row. Same streets. Different names. Same people? No. Different story." A girl named Nia raised her hand. "So, gentrification is just—what? A slow war?" Ms. Hollis nodded. "Exactly. A war fought with leases instead of bullets." The door upstairs slammed open.
The room fell silent.

Heavy boots pounded the floor above—fast, tactical, deliberate.

Then came the voice, mechanical and cruel through a megaphone: "This is a federal operation. All unauthorized occupants must remain where they are. Hands visible. Resistance will be met with force." The lights flickered.

Ms. Hollis moved calmly. "Down. Back wall. Emergency protocol." The kids didn't cry. They didn't scream. They'd been drilled for this. Behind the supply cabinet was a false panel. Behind that, a narrow crawlspace lined with soundproofing insulation and emergency water rations. One by one, they slid in. Ms. Hollis waited until the last student had disappeared. Then she turned off the projector and laid her chalk on the floor in an X pattern.

By the time the Memory Crimes Unit broke through the basement doors, she was seated calmly at her desk, reading from A People's History of the United States.

Agent Charlene Wexler led the team. Helmeted. Gloved. Laser-focused.

"Put the book down."

Ms. Hollis looked up, her voice even.

"Which one, Agent?"

Wexler didn't answer. Her team swept the room—kicking open supply cabinets, scanning walls, seizing devices. They found a locked trunk and forced it open. Inside: handwritten journals, flash drives taped to crayon boxes, photocopied syllabi hidden inside false hymnals. Wexler picked up one booklet.

Reading the Riot Act: A Community Syllabus on Rebellion and Resistance.

She shook her head.

"Subversive. Anti-American. Dangerous."

Ms. Hollis raised an eyebrow. "Which part? The part where it tells them to ask questions? Or the part where it teaches them to read maps?"

Wexler turned away.

"Bag it all. This site's contaminated."

Outside, a government drone hovered over the church as armored vans arrived.

Within an hour, the basement was emptied.

Books confiscated. Equipment seized. The chalk X scrubbed away.

The walls were left bare.

But they didn't find the crawlspace. They didn't hear the whispers. And they didn't see the backup drive that had already uploaded everything to three other nodes across the country. Far away, in a safehouse in Detroit, Langston watched the raid footage on a private stream. His fingers pressed into the wood of his desk as the screen froze on Agent Wexler's face.

He said nothing.

But behind him, Dr. Rojas whispered, "It's started."

Langston nodded once.

"Then we move to Phase Three." Langston knew this raid wouldn't go unanswered.

The next battle would not be in basements.

It would be broadcast.

Chapter 7: Confronting the Doctrine

The studio lights were warm and deceitful. Langston adjusted his collar and looked into the black glass of the camera lens. Across from him, separated by less than ten feet of laminate flooring but an ocean of ideology, sat Charles Norrington. Draped in a tailored navy suit, crisp white pocket square, and his trademark eagle-and-key lapel pin, Norrington leaned back in his chair with the ease of a man who believed the narrative already belonged to him.

The segment was billed as a "national conversation on educational integrity." Langston knew better. It was an ambush—carefully framed, heavily edited, preloaded with rhetoric. The host, a platinum-haired anchor with the smile of a crocodile, began: "With us tonight: Mr. Charles Norrington, author of the American Priorities Doctrine, and Dr. Langston Graham, founder of the controversial ScholarForge network. Gentlemen, let's begin." Norrington struck first. "ScholarForge is not education. It's a soft insurgency. A decentralized machine spreading anti-American sentiment under the guise of literacy." Langston didn't flinch. "If teaching unredacted history is rebellion," he said calmly, "then maybe you should ask why your version of patriotism demands so much forgetting." The anchor shifted.

"Dr. Graham, do you deny ScholarForge has operated outside official accreditation?"

"Absolutely not," Langston said. "Accreditation requires compliance with curriculum mandates that erase Reconstruction, downplay redlining, and call enslavement an 'economic migration.' We operate outside of that because truth lives outside of that."

Norrington leaned forward. "Truth is not subjective. America is a nation built on order. When you undermine order, you invite chaos." Langston turned his gaze toward him— measured, but unmistakably lethal. "No, sir. America was built on property— and Black lives were categorized as such. That's not order. That's cruelty made bureaucratic." The studio went silent. "You say we invite chaos. But your mandates revive it. Gutting DEI. Militarizing borders. Silencing educators. You're not draining a swamp—you're drowning truth." The anchor tried to pivot. "Surely you agree that we need a unifying curriculum to preserve national cohesion." Langston shook his head slowly. "Cohesion at the cost of reality is propaganda. And propaganda is how you prepare a population for tyranny." Norrington's voice lost its polish for a beat.

"We're restoring American values." Langston leaned in now, calm as thunder. "The last time someone said that my grandfather lost his job for organizing a union. Before that, my great-grandmother

was beaten for teaching freedmen how to read. Your 'values' are a river of recycled mandates, sir. We've seen them before."
The timer blinked red. Segment almost over.
The anchor looked rattled.
Langston turned to the camera directly.
"To the students watching—know this: You are not confused. You are not angry without reason. You are inheriting a war that started centuries ago.
And if remembering makes you dangerous— Be dangerous. Be precise. And be unafraid." The feed cut.
Outside the studio, reporters swarmed. Inside online message boards, the hashtag had already gone viral:
#MandatesAreNotMemory
#LangstonWasRight
In a bunker outside Philadelphia, a young coder tapped the words into a ScholarForge broadcast interface and smiled.
Across the bottom of the stream, Langston's final words appeared in bold type:
"Memory is not the enemy of progress. Amnesia is."

Chapter 8: The Counter Code

Marcus Baker sat hunched in a sub-level ScholarForge terminal pod, three stories beneath what had once been a teacher training center in Atlanta. Above ground, it was now a sterile "AI Curriculum Calibration Facility." Below ground, it was something else: a digital no-man's land littered with broken patches of archived knowledge and buried memory protocols. He adjusted the security mirror he had wired into the corner—his only defense against random biometric sweeps. The interface before him pulsed: blue lines of corrupted learning models, white boxes marking banned data clusters. He inserted the drive Monroe had sent. The terminal stuttered. Then it opened.

FILE REBUILD — PHASE I: HOPE LEDGER MANDATES RE-INJECTION — AUTH CODE: GRAHAM/CRUMMELL

Marcus wiped his hands on his jeans. He didn't speak as the documents rendered line by line—John Hope's original mandates, and then the suppressed audio logs from Washington. But what brought him pause was the additional set Monroe had flagged: The Crummell Dispatches. Rare writings. Encrypted text. Philosophical essays that had never made it into most textbooks, much less machine learning repositories. One line surfaced and locked on-screen:

"What you do for yourself alone dies with you; what you do for others, and the world remains and is immortal."
— Alexander Crummell

Marcus whispered it aloud, just to feel its shape.

Crummell had known the weight of moral duty. A Black intellectual exiled to Liberia because America had no room for his genius. But he'd returned with fire. Now, that same fire blinked in Marcus's hands. He tapped into ScholarForge's hidden logic layer—Core Node-12, a remnant built years earlier by Langston himself. At the core of the system's moral logic circuits was something few remembered: the Langston Condition. It could only be rewritten from inside the system, and only by a voice that echoed its foundational syntax.

A second quote flashed onto the screen, buried in an older programming string Langston had authored during his time in development:

"As long as I live, and until the last hour of my breath, I shall strive for the cause of the people." — John Mercer Langston

Marcus froze.

The system responded to Langston's name not just as a user—but as a variable.

[ROOT VARIABLE:
MERCER_LANGSTON = "civic

sovereignty / narrative integrity"] Marcus realized what Langston had done. ScholarForge wasn't just a curriculum engine. It was a time capsule. And he had hidden the key inside the language of two ancestors whose names he bore in spirit.

He opened a new editor window, voice coding into the system:

"Reinstate Hope Ledger. Inject Crummell Ethics Framework. Bind under Langston Condition." The cursor blinked.

Then—

"Mandates restored. Core resistance node reactivated."

The lights in the pod dimmed slightly. Not in error—but in confirmation. He had done it.

And then, just before closing the interface, he added one final quote into the ScholarForge user onboarding protocol—a phrase that would greet every student AI interface in the next deployment cycle:

"We must never forget that education is not merely a means to life—it is life itself."

— Alexander Crummell

He leaned back and let out a long breath. The counter code had been written. Now the real work would begin.

Chapter 9: The Forbidden Module

The ScholarForge interface pulsed quietly inside Langston Graham's manor office. It was late. Jane Monroe stood by the window, watching the storm clouds roll over the treetops, her gloved hands clasped behind her back. She had not spoken since Marcus sent confirmation that the Hope Ledger and Crummell protocols had taken root in the system. Langston leaned closer to the screen. The latest patch logs were displaying anomalies—code branches forming outside their original permissions. One line read:
INJECTION DETECTED: MODULE— J.H. CLARKE / CLASSIFIED AS "NON-COMPLIANT MEMORY"
His brow furrowed.
Monroe turned from the window. "They're already trying to shut it down?" "No," Langston said. "This isn't suppression. It's resurrection." He opened the module. A video began to play—grainy footage from 1987. John Henrik Clarke sat behind a wooden podium, his voice firm, eyes like steel behind thick-rimmed glasses. "Power is the ability to define history and have that definition accepted by others." Langston froze. He knew the quote. He'd written it on the inside flap of his first journal in grad school. But hearing it now—buried inside ScholarForge, tagged "non-compliant"—was something else. Clarke continued:

"If you are not careful, the textbooks you trust will convince you that your oppressor is your savior, and your hero is your enemy."

The video flickered, then stopped.

WARNING: USER ATTEMPTING TO ACCESS BANNED INTELLECTUAL PROPERTY. RESTRICTION CODE: PATRIOT RE-ALIGNMENT ORDER 3.1.7

Langston stood slowly.

"They're not just erasing him," he said. "They've labeled him a threat to national alignment."

Monroe spoke gently. "Then perhaps that's how we know we're on the right path."

Langston moved to a secure drawer, removed a slim black data drive marked SWORD 2. He slotted it in. The system asked for his biometric override. He placed his hand on the scanner.

ADMIN OVERRIDE ACCEPTED. ENABLE—CLARKE PROTOCOL?

He clicked Yes.

Then, in a calm voice, he gave a single command:

"Begin counter-narrative loop. Inject Dr. Clarke's opening lecture on Pan-African contributions to Western Civilization into all Level 3 civics modules." The system blinked.

INJECTION COMPLETE. ESTIMATED TIME TO FLAG: 11 HOURS.

Langston turned to Monroe. "That gives us one school day."

"Enough to open eyes," she replied.

Langston nodded. "Let the students meet

the teacher they were never supposed to
know."

*"Power is the ability to define history and
have that definition accepted by others."*

— Dr. John Henrik Clarke

ScholarForge Address — Internal Use
Only

Dr. Graham stood at the head of the long
oak table, clad in a midnight Brooks
Brothers three-piece—understated and
impeccable. The only glint beyond the
polished lapel pin was the worn gold
signet ring on his left hand, carved with
the ScholarForge seal and the inscription:
Veritas Vincit — Truth Prevails.

"Ladies and gentlemen…

The fact that we are gathered here—
quietly, off the record, away from the eyes
of press or party—speaks volumes.

You are here not because you want to look
good.
You are here because you finally want to
see clearly.

Let me begin with what must be said
plainly:

Truth does not wear a race. It is not
Black, white, brown, or yellow. It does
not answer to your political party or align
itself with your upbringing. Truth doesn't
bow to profit margins. It doesn't obey

poll numbers. Truth is what remains
when every convenient lie has been
burned away.

I wear this ring not as decoration— but
as obligation.

It was forged in secrecy and passed
through generations like a lit fuse—quiet,
hot, dangerous to the careless. It does
not shine because it is gold. It shines
because it has survived.

And you—those of you seated here—are
now part of what it protects.

Some of your ancestors helped shape the
very systems ScholarForge now works to
subvert. Others tried to stop it and were
silenced. And some of you… some of you
only just opened your eyes last year.

That does not matter.
What matters is what you do next.

You do not sit here as heroes. You
sit here as witnesses.

Witnesses to the greatest lie ever told:
That education can be neutral.
That history can be negotiated. That
memory can be managed.

ScholarForge is not here to be palatable. It
is here to be precise.
And we accept your gifts, your wiring
instructions, your quiet endowments…

But understand this: You are not
funding a school. You are funding a
reckoning.

You are funding the restoration of memory
stolen across generations. You are planting
truth in soil your ancestors may have
poisoned. And still— what grows from it
may heal this land.

Because truth—if allowed to breathe—
redeems everyone it touches.

And so, I wear this ring, carved with the
ScholarForge seal, not to honor myself—

But to remember the teachers who taught
behind curtains.
The elders who read by candlelight when
the law denied them literacy. The
children who memorized forbidden lines
of Frederick Douglass while pretending
to practice arithmetic.

This ring is a promise. And
now, so are you.

Because if you've made it this far, you
have already left behind the world of
neutrality.

You are now keepers of a flame you didn't
light… but that you must never let die.

Welcome to the Forge.

Chapter 10: A Mind Honed Like Steel

The storm had passed. Morning light spilled through the bay windows of the manor's study, touching the mahogany shelves that lined the room. Langston Graham sat at his writing desk in a dark waistcoat, surrounded by letters, old manuscripts, and one still-open ScholarForge terminal. Marcus Baker sat opposite him. He had bags under his eyes, the result of two nights spent rebuilding what had been shattered. But his hands were steady. His eyes alert. Langston poured a cup of strong Kenyan coffee and handed it to Marcus without a word.

"I saw what you did," Langston said finally. "You used the Langston Condition to stabilize the Hope Ledger and injected the Clarke module under trace delay." Marcus gave a nod. "It worked." Langston studied him for a long moment. "Yes. And because it worked, you've placed yourself squarely in their sights. So now you must ask: what kind of man are you becoming?" Marcus raised an eyebrow. "What kind?" "Power is not just access to data. It's the ability to remain intact when the world tries to rewrite you." Langston stood and walked to the bookcase, pulling out a worn leatherbound volume.

"The Souls of Black Folk," he said, holding it up. "Du Bois didn't just write theory—he wrote armor. That's why they ban it. That's why they call it 'radical.'

Because it tells you that to be Black and conscious in America is to walk with double vision—and not lose your balance."

He opened to a page and handed the book to Marcus.

"One ever feels his two-ness, —an American, a Negro; two souls, two thoughts, two unreconciled strivings…" Marcus read it aloud. "…two warring ideals in one dark body."

Langston nodded. "Du Bois didn't give us easy answers. He gave us a blueprint for dignity under pressure. That's what you'll need."

Marcus leaned forward. "But he also believed in the Talented Tenth. Isn't that elitist?"

Langston smiled. "No. That's what his critics misunderstood. He wasn't saying only the Tenth mattered. He was saying the Tenth must be ready—trained, fortified, morally grounded. Not to rule, but to lift. To remember. To serve the ninety."

Before Marcus could respond, Monroe entered quietly from the west corridor with a discreet clipboard in hand. "Your delivery from Brooks Brothers arrived, Dr. Graham," she said. "One dozen white, one dozen blue, one dozen pink, button-down oxfords—just as specified."

Langston nodded, then glanced briefly toward the armoire.

"Please remind the cleaning staff to have the previous set boxed and donated to

Goodwill," he added, "they're still in excellent condition."

"Of course," Monroe replied, her voice smooth as polished marble. Langston turned back to Marcus. "Presentation is not performance. It's code. It tells the world that you curate yourself with care, not approval." Marcus gave a quiet, thoughtful nod. Langston returned to the desk and opened a drawer, pulling out a small, cloth covered notebook. "Then you start your own," he said. Marcus took the journal, eyes widening slightly. The cover bore a single, embossed word:

REMEMBER.

Chapter 11: Echoes and Entrances

Marcus sat alone in the manor's west reading room, the cloth-bound journal open before him. The word REMEMBER embossed on its cover seemed to shimmer in the morning light, like a quiet command more than a title.

He had written only one line so far: If memory is a weapon, then this will be my sword.

But the next words didn't come easily. His thoughts were clouded—not by doubt, but by something more personal. Guilt. Distance. Fear.

He pulled out his phone and checked for messages. Still, none from Aunt Pam. She had missed his last two calls. Her caretaker said she was resting more lately, but Marcus knew what that meant. Rest was a soft euphemism for decline. She had raised him after his mother passed, working overnight shifts in a hospital kitchen so he could attend a charter school that didn't see him as a statistic. She never asked for praise. Just a weekly phone call. And now, at the moment of his greatest intellectual calling, Marcus felt like he was abandoning the person who had first taught him what quiet dignity looked like.

He rubbed his temples. The revolution was happening—and he was in it—but his heart was 300 miles away, in a two bedroom apartment in Norfolk where Aunt

Pam kept Du Bois on her nightstand and gospel vinyls in a crate marked "STAYING POWER."

A knock at the side door broke his reverie. It opened slowly, and in stepped Sabrina Graham.

She was taller than Marcus expected, elegant in movement, wearing a navy silk blouse and pearl earrings, her hair natural and regal. She carried no clipboard, no laptop—only presence.

"You must be Marcus," she said warmly. "I'm Sabrina."

Marcus stood, instinctively straightening his shoulders.

"Yes, ma'am."

She smiled gently. "I'm not that old, child."

They both chuckled. Then she nodded toward the journal.

"Langston used to write letters to his father in his first notebooks. Not to send—just to sort things out. I'm guessing you're in that phase?"

Marcus hesitated. "Something like that. It's… it's my aunt. She's not well. She raised me."

Sabrina's expression softened. "She poured into you so you could pour into the world. But don't confuse purpose with distance. Call her. Even if it's just to say you haven't forgotten." Marcus swallowed and nodded. "Yes, ma'am. I mean—yes. I will." She walked to the bookshelves and ran her fingers lightly across the spines. "You'll find that Langston builds defenses with words and ideas. But he forgets that sometimes, people need presence too. That's why I stay close."

Marcus glanced toward the study down the hall, where Langston was once again deep in research.

Sabrina turned to leave but paused. "When you write tonight," she said, "don't just write about theory or rebellion. Write about her—your aunt. Because no matter what you build here, it started in her kitchen."

Then she was gone.

Marcus sat again. The page waited. He picked up the pen, drew a deep breath, and began to write:

Aunt Pam, you always said to be ready when history knocked. I thought it would sound like drums. Turns out, it sounds like silence and a chance to speak…

Chapter 12: What They Gave Us

Marcus stood on the balcony just outside the west library, phone pressed to his ear, the wind tugging gently at his collar. The sky had turned gray again—clouds hanging low, as if mourning something the world hadn't yet acknowledged. The phone rang three times before a quiet voice answered.
It wasn't his aunt.
It was her nurse.
A pause.
Then, gently: "She passed early this morning, baby. Peaceful. She had your letter from last week folded in her hand."
A sound escaped him, quiet and sharp.
Grief didn't wail—it settled. Heavy. Inevitable.
He said thank you. His voice cracked.
Then he hung up and stayed there for a long time, gripping the iron railing as if it could anchor him to something solid.
Below, the wind rustled the hedges.

Langston Graham watched from the study window.
He said nothing when Marcus returned, only slid a second cup of coffee across the desk and waited.
Marcus sat slowly. His eyes were open, but distant.
"She's gone," he said. "Aunt Pam."
Langston nodded once and folded his hands.

Marcus exhaled. "She used to iron my school clothes while listening to gospel music and talking back to the radio. Always Mahalia Jackson and Nina Simone in the same breath. She made me read Baldwin before I was tall enough to ride roller coasters."

A thin smile touched his lips, then broke. "She called it 'mental armor.' Said the world would try to strip me down before I even knew I was dressed." Langston leaned back slightly, letting the moment settle.

"My grandmother—Patty—was the same," he said. "Except she'd watch me shine my shoes. Wouldn't do it for me. Just sat in the doorway and said, 'If your shoes are shined, Langston, they can't say you were raised wrong—even if they treat you like you were.' I must've polished a thousand shoes before I understood what she was really teaching me." Marcus looked up. "They never said much, huh?"

Langston chuckled softly. "No. But they taught everything."

He reached into a drawer and pulled out a folded photograph—aged but preserved. A young Langston, no older than fifteen, standing in front of The Roger Gardens housing project in Trenton. Grandma Patty beside him, her hand on his shoulder, her posture regal in a plain blue dress.

"They didn't teach us to be loud," Langston said. "They taught us to be clear. They knew what the world would try to make of us, so they left no part of us untouched. They baked the lessons into the small things—how to fold a towel, how to enter a room, how to speak when the stakes were high, and your dignity was the only currency you had left." Marcus nodded slowly, eyes misting. "She gave up so much," he said. "Never had a vacation. Never had a new car. But she made me feel like I was worth the whole world." Langston looked at him with a solemn steadiness.

"You were. And you still are. And if you want to honor her, you don't just mourn. You build. You outthink the ones trying to reduce you. You carry her memory in how you work, how you dress, how you walk into rooms they thought you'd never enter."

Marcus wiped his face and laughed gently. "She always told me to keep my collar straight. Said 'people will judge you by your shoes and your bookshelves.'" Langston nodded. "Then she and Patty would've gotten along just fine." He leaned forward.

"Let me give you something that won't fit in a textbook, Marcus. This is advice for the road ahead: Live in a way that makes the people who bet against you feel like they were speaking a different language. Let dignity be your signature. Let memory be your discipline. Let her sacrifice be your blueprint."

The room went still.

Then Marcus said, "Thank you, Dr. Graham. For not just the work—but for the quiet things."

Langston placed a hand on his shoulder. "You don't need to be perfect, son. But you damn sure better be prepared."

Redacted File: The Pause Between Notes

The Mercedes Benz glided out of Graham Manor's private gate with the smooth hum of German engineering and a quiet dignity. The sky was overcast, a soft gray pressing against the leafy canopy that shaded the manicured lanes of the suburban enclave. Dr. Langston Elkanah Graham adjusted the volume knob gently, letting the mellow syncopation of *Take Five* by the Dave Brubeck Quartet fill the cabin like silk.

Marcus sat in the passenger seat, flipping absently through notifications on his phone, but the rhythm of the jazz tune seemed to interrupt even the algorithm's tyranny. As they passed the last circle of manicured lawns, Langston's eyes drifted to the road ahead. The scenery was beginning to shift—from tailored hedges and iron fences to cracked sidewalks and sagging utility poles.

At the red light on North Lexington, they slowed to a full stop. There, standing on the narrow median with a cardboard sign smeared in fading marker, was a man wrapped in a green Army surplus coat. His beard was overgrown, his face weathered and raw. He didn't speak. He just held the sign.

"Anything helps. God bless."
Langston reached into the side compartment for a folded bill. Marcus

sighed, annoyed. "I wish you'd stop doing this."

Langston raised an eyebrow but didn't respond immediately.

"You don't know what he's going to do with that money," Marcus continued. "These guys might be scammers or con artists. They play on your guilt. You don't even know if he's really homeless."

Langston eased the car into park and turned the music down just slightly. The light remained red.

He looked over at Marcus. "In a little while, we'll be driving back home. You'll eat, maybe read, then call it a night. I'll spend some time with Sabrina and then turn in." We are fortunate on many levels.

Marcus shifted in his seat.

Langston held out the bill through the cracked window. The man approached quietly, took the money with a silent nod of thanks, and stepped back just as the light turned green.

Langston continued. "Tell me—who am I to deny this man food? A sandwich, a cup of coffee, a bus ticket—whatever it may be. How is it that in the richest country in the history of the world, there are people hungry and without shelter? We give billion-dollar subsidies to industries, write off yachts and private jets, and then tell ourselves the lie that helping the poor is bad economics."

The Mercedes merged back into traffic. The song looped again—Joe Morello's drum solo building quietly under Paul Desmond's smooth sax.

Langston's voice dropped to a near whisper.

"What's truly vile, Marcus, isn't just the poverty—it's the way we blame the poor for being poor. As if they chose to suffer. As if it's moral failure, not policy and cruelty, that landed them there."

Marcus didn't respond immediately. He looked back through the rearview mirror, watching the shrinking figure of the man disappear into the distance.

The car moved on. But the moment hung in the air like the space between jazz notes—unexpected, unresolved, and deeply human.

Marcus exhaled through his nose, tapping his fingers against the door panel as if trying to drum away the discomfort. "But don't you ever feel like we're enabling something? I mean, I get it, I do—but where's the line between helping and being played?"
Langston didn't answer right away. He adjusted the steering wheel slightly and turned onto Albemarle, the city creeping up in jagged contrast to the harmony of the

music. The jazz wasn't just background noise—it was metaphor, movement, message.

"I've studied a lot of lines in my life," Langston said finally. "Lines in legislation. Lines in redlined neighborhoods. Lines of credit denied. Lines drawn in courtrooms and classrooms and city council meetings. Funny how we always find our precision when it comes to denying someone else mercy."

Marcus shifted again, this time uncomfortably. "You always turn this into something bigger."

"Because it is," Langston said gently. "Because that man—who you assume might be gaming the system—*is* the system. He is its byproduct, its consequence. He is what happens when safety nets become nooses. When politics is more interested in punishment than people."

The traffic thickened. Horns barked in the distance. A siren moaned from somewhere behind them, weaving through the city like a ghost unsure of where to land. Langston tapped the steering wheel once. "You know why I give?" he said. "Not because I think I'm saving anyone. I'm not that arrogant. I give because if I start deciding who's worthy of compassion, I've become the very thing I claim to stand against."

Marcus said nothing, but the silence between them wasn't empty—it was consideration, like the breath a musician takes before hitting the note that makes the whole piece matter.

They passed a mural painted on the side of a bodega: *Feed the People, Heal the Land.* The colors had faded, but the message remained bold.

Langston glanced at it, then back at the road. "Justice, Marcus, is jazz. It's not always neat. It doesn't follow the rules you expect. But it moves. And sometimes, the most important part isn't the note—it's the pause between them."

Marcus turned to look at him, the corners of his mouth pressing into a reluctant, contemplative line.

The Benz rolled forward, smooth as silk and heavy with meaning, leaving behind a city that had forgotten its own pauses.

Chapter 13: The Hedge Around Him

Langston was lucky. Or at least, that's what folks said.

In a city where boys his age were often swallowed whole by the streets—by corner hustlers with open palms and hollow promises, by gang recruiters dressed like big brothers, by the quiet hum of temptation that crept in every shadow—Langston somehow managed to move untouched. Not invincible, not invisible, but… protected.

He wasn't immune to bullying. The schoolyard still tested him. There were still shoves in the hallway, whispers behind backs, knuckles too eager to prove something. But the deeper vices—the ones that rewired your future before your voice had even changed—those seemed to skip over him like a skipped stone refusing to sink.

Maybe it was Troop 340, a band of misfits and dreamers tucked into a backroom with squeaky chairs and lukewarm lemonade. There, in the scratchy polyester of a scout uniform, Langston learned how to tie

knots, start fires, pitch tents, and recite the
Scout Law like scripture: trustworthy,
loyal, helpful, friendly… Somewhere
between the badge ceremonies and
camping trips, he learned about honor
from men who had never been honored
but carried dignity in their gait like
something inherited.

Or maybe it was Jade Dragon's Karate,
and the cracked vinyl mats that soaked up
the sweat and grit of neighborhood kids
with more to prove than they could say.
Langston still remembered the coolness of
the floor on bare feet, the rhythmic thud of
punches against pads, and the way the
instructor would say, "Discipline is a
decision, not a feeling." Each kata, each
sparring round, became a quiet rebellion
against chaos. He didn't know it then, but
every front kick was a message to the
world: I will not fall easily.

It definitely wasn't the youth choir.
Langston hated that. He remembered
standing stiff in the second row of robes,
mouthing the words more than singing
them, eyes locked on the back door,
praying for escape. Sister Geraldine
would hiss, "Open your mouth, boy, the
Lord gave you a voice," and he'd mutter
under his breath, Then He should've kept
it in a box. Being an altar boy was
tolerable. There was dignity in lighting
candles, in folding hands just so, in
ringing the bell with precise timing. And
there was power, too—in being close to
the pulpit, to the stories, to the echoes of
men who made scripture sound like

thunder. Langston didn't know it then, but he was learning cadence, poise, and how to read a room.

But above all, it was Patty Crocker. His grandmother.

The quiet architect of his shield. She never called it a hedge of protection, though she prayed one around him every morning. She just called it "doing what needed doing."

When the Scout dues came due—$18 for the uniform shirt, $12 for the handbook, and something for snacks—she found it. Quietly. Sometimes by pawning an old brooch or skipping the bus to work and walking the extra miles to save the fare. When the karate school fees crept up— testing fees, tournament gear, dobok replacements—she didn't flinch. She'd just nod and say, "We'll handle it," then figure out how. If that meant borrowing from the church benevolence fund, she'd do it. If it meant calling folks she'd rather not call and asking for rides—knowing full well the look they'd give her, the pity that stung like vinegar—she'd do that, too. Every sacrifice she made chipped a little piece from her pride, but she never let Langston see her sweat.

She fed him purpose with every meal. *"Baby,"* she once told him while heating beans on the stove, *"there's people who gon' try and hand you a life that ain't yours to live. Don't let nobody sign you up for sorrow."*

He was twelve when she said that. Too young to understand the weight of her words, but old enough to feel the love wrapped in them.

Years later, when his peers talked about the first time they smoked, the first time they ran from blue lights, the first time they felt the cold steel of a cell lock, Langston would think of Patty. Of the hedge she built, brick by weary brick. Invisible to most, but strong enough to redirect a destiny.

He wasn't better than the others. Just… blessed by a woman who refused to let the streets have him.

And when people praised his calm, his conviction, his clarity—Langston never pretended it came from nowhere. He remembered the beans on the stove, the smell of mothballs and prayer oil, the ache in Patty's knees and the steel in her voice.

He signed his own name.

And beneath it, in invisible ink, was hers.

Chapter 14: Ink and Earth

The cemetery sat just off a country road outside Norfolk. Nothing fancy—no iron gates or mausoleums. Just a gentle slope, rows of headstones, and a large oak that shaded the corner plot where Pam Baker had been laid to rest.
Marcus stood alone. He wore a navy blazer, soft in the shoulders, paired with a crisp white oxford shirt. The outfit came from a local consignment shop—clean, timeless, and chosen with care. Aunt Pam would've approved. She had always believed that elegance wasn't about the label, but about how you carried yourself in it. In his hand, he held a single flower. Not roses. A hydrangea. Her favorite. "Because they never need too much to be beautiful," she used to say. The sky was a soft blue. Windless. Still. He knelt and placed the flower carefully beside the headstone, fingers brushing the engraving:
Pamela R. Baker 1961–2025
She loved deeply and taught in silence. Marcus stayed there a while, eyes closed, remembering the warmth of her kitchen, the scent of fried okra, the sound of Mahalia Jackson floating from the radio, and the way she always made enough food for whoever might stop by—even when they never did.
But today wasn't just about Aunt Pam.
It was about all of them.
The aunts who took in nephews like sons.
The mothers who went without so their

children could go beyond. The grandmothers who held families together with iron will and soft hands. Women who ignored their own dreams so their children could dream bigger. Women who were never asked what they wanted— only expected to endure.
And they did.

Marcus stood not just to honor one woman, but a generation of women who had lived for legacy, not comfort. Who had sacrificed happiness for strength, believing that if the next generation could walk with their heads held high, maybe that was joy enough.
He didn't cry. Not because he couldn't. But because something steadier had settled in him now.
Resolve.
That evening, back at Graham Manor, he sat by the window of the west study. A gift from Langston lay before him: a leatherbound Moroccan journal—dark burgundy, hand-stitched, with a braided leather strap to close it.
There were three of them in the box. "In case one life can't hold all your thoughts," Langston had said with a half-smile.
Marcus opened the first. He ran his fingers over the grain of the page, then began to write.
This time, the words came freely. Today I buried the woman who taught me the difference between being smart and being steady.

She taught me that dignity isn't what you demand—it's what you refuse to surrender. That education was never about applause. It was armor.

That no matter how far I go, I take her hands with me. Her silence. Her Sunday shirts. Her food that tasted like grace. And when I rise, I do so in the name of all the women who bent low so we could stand tall.

He paused, then added one last line: They took her body. But they'll never unteach what she taught me. He closed the journal gently, wrapping the strap once around. Across the room, Langston's study door was slightly ajar. Warm light spilled out across the polished floor. Marcus sat still for a long moment. Then stood.

He straightened his collar. The world would try again tomorrow. And he would be ready. But now, he remembered the words: 'Let memory be your discipline.

Chapter 15: The Lesson They Can't Ban

From Marcus's journal:

Governments may ban programs and remove artifacts, but they can never erase what's already been read, remembered, and passed down. Our true history lives in our books, our minds, and the lessons we teach each other when no one else is watching.

The classroom smelled like dry erase markers and ambition.
Located in a quiet wing of the Southern Piedmont Educational Center—one of the last publicly-funded learning labs partnered with ScholarForge—Room 2B had been designated for "elective enrichment." Translation: a forgotten space for students who didn't test into the top-tier data streams but hadn't yet been labeled disengaged.
It was perfect.
Marcus stood at the whiteboard, notebook in hand, the Moroccan leather journal tucked beneath a copy of The Souls of Black Folk. Six students sat before him— three seniors, two juniors, and a sophomore. Black and brown. Curious, guarded, sharp-eyed. They hadn't signed

up for a lecture. They came because
Marcus had told one student, "I'll show
you what they won't teach you." And
word had spread.
He clicked on the terminal.
The ScholarForge screen blinked to life.
For a moment, the default interface
loaded—sterile and sanitized. But then,
quietly, the system shifted. Marcus entered
a private protocol built into Langston's
override. The screen flickered once more.
A hidden archive loaded.
At the top: The Clarke Lectures
Below that: Hope Ledger Ethics
And underneath: Crummell's Memory
Doctrine — Unabridged He looked at
the students. "Before we start, I want
you to know this isn't about rebellion."
A hand went up. "It kinda feels like it is."

Marcus smiled. "Maybe it's better to
say… It's about remembrance. Because
forgetting has never been neutral. It's been
policy."
He opened Du Bois's book, flipped to the
first essay, and read aloud: "The Nation
has not yet found peace from its sins; the
freedman has not yet found in freedom
his promised land." He paused. "Anyone
ever seen that in your history
module?" Heads
shook.
He closed the book.
"That's the problem."
They worked for two hours. No tests. No
filters. Just real names. Real lives. They
listened to Dr. John Henrik Clarke's 1987

lecture on African civilizations contributing to Western science and philosophy. They traced lines between Clarke's critique of Eurocentric history and modern AI training sets. Marcus connected it to ScholarForge's new "contextualized patriotism" filter—a setting that automatically flagged content critical of U.S. foreign policy or systemic injustice.

"So, the AI's racist?" one student asked. Marcus shook his head. "Not on its own. It's trained to be… agreeable. The racism is in the hands that told it what to ignore." They leaned in after that.

Around noon, Monroe arrived quietly with a tray of sandwiches and fruit cups. She wore a simple navy blazer, her presence graceful and reserved. She placed the tray at the back of the room without interrupting.

Marcus glanced at her with gratitude. She gave a subtle nod before exiting just as quietly.

After lunch, they turned to Alexander Crummell.

Marcus projected the quote:

"The dignity of a people can never be preserved through the forgetting of its past."

The students copied it by hand. Marcus didn't tell them to.

One girl asked, "Why don't we ever hear about him?"

"Because dignity," Marcus said, "is harder to market than guilt."

At the end of the session, Marcus handed
out blank index cards.
"Write one thing you learned today that
you want to carry with you," he said.
"Something you won't find in your official
curriculum." They
wrote in silence.
One card read:
"History is not what happened. It's what
survived." Another:
"I didn't know we built universities in
Timbuktu." A third:
"I want to make my grandma proud with
what I remember."
Marcus collected them all. He read each
one, slowly. Then placed them in his
journal, between two empty pages.

That evening, back at the manor, he joined
Langston in the study.
Langston looked up from his desk, where
a series of redacted reports on
ScholarForge's compliance protocols were
scattered like forensic evidence.
"Well?" he asked.
"They showed up," Marcus said. "Not just
physically. Mentally. They listened."
Langston leaned back, his expression
unreadable.
"They're still out there, you know.
Watching."

"I know," Marcus replied. "But so are
we." Langston reached across the desk
and handed him a folder.

Inside was a memo from the State Office of Digital Integrity. The subject line read: INTERNAL ALERT: Unsupervised ScholarForge Material Detected — CLASSIFICATION: NON-COMPLIANT MEMORY MODULES

Langston met his eyes. "It's begun."

Marcus closed the folder.

"Then let's begin with them."

Chapter 16: History They Can't Unteach

From Marcus's Journal: "History is dangerous when the truth names names. Especially when the names are in your government, your deeds, and your denial."

The bell had rung five minutes ago, but no one in Room 2B moved. The lights were dimmed, the digital terminal active, and The Color of Law sat in the center of the table like contraband in plain sight. Marcus stood beside it, a quiet gravity in his voice.

"This book tells you something you're not supposed to know, that segregation wasn't a Southern accident or 'natural sorting.' It was national policy—built into housing codes, zoning laws, and mortgage agreements."

He flipped to a flagged page.

"Here—1949, Levittown, Pennsylvania. An entire suburb built with federal support, but no Black families allowed. FHA rules required that homes be sold only to white buyers. That's not a suggestion. That's law."

Langston, reading the surveillance report later that night, paused at the name. Levittown.

He remembered being eleven years old, sitting in a too-small desk at Stokes School in Trenton, New Jersey. His sixth grade teacher, Mr. Riche always arrived sharply dressed and drove in each morning from Levittown. He never said why he didn't live nearby. Langston had always wondered why a teacher who smiled so easily seemed to live a life so far removed from the blocks he walked each day. He turned to the screen. A HUD map of Charlotte blinked into view—historic redlining in high contrast. "The red zones on this map? That's where African Americans were permitted to live—if at all. No loans, no investment, no infrastructure."

A hand went up—Elijah, a soft-spoken junior with sharp eyes and a hoodie that said My Existence Is Political. "But this was decades ago, right? Why does it still matter?"

Marcus tapped the keyboard. The map dissolved into a side-by-side of modern-day Charlotte and the 1940s redlining zones.

"Because these same redlined neighborhoods are still the ones with underfunded schools. Still the ones where home values are lowest. Still the ones where families rent, not own." He turned back to Elijah. "So, while white families were buying homes and building equity— passing that wealth down generation after generation— Black families were blocked. That's not just inequality. That's generational theft." Another hand rose— Mari, a senior who rarely spoke unless she meant it. "My mom's been renting the same apartment for twenty years. Same block my grandmother lived on. Every year the rent goes up, and we get nothing back. No savings, no ownership." Marcus nodded solemnly.

"That's the legacy. You don't pass down a lease. You pass down land. And when a whole people are locked out of ownership? You don't just lose money—you lose power, protection, and peace of mind." He clicked again. A chart appeared: median family wealth by race. White families: $188,200

Black families: $24,100 Latino families: $36,100 Gasps.

"This," Marcus said, "isn't about hustle. It's about access. And when your grandparents weren't allowed to buy property, your parents were forced to rent, and you start life behind, hard work becomes survival, not stability." He let the silence breathe.

"And don't let them twist the narrative," Marcus added. "These politicians want you to believe that diversity is an affront to justice—something forced or unfair. But the truth is, it's the injustice that made programs like DEI necessary in the first place. Equity isn't a handout. It's a correction."

"That's why books like The Color of Law are being pulled from classrooms. Because they don't just expose racism. They expose receipts."

Monroe entered quietly with a tray of paper cups and water bottles. Her blazer crisp, posture erect, presence composed. She whispered, "Surveillance in the portal is active again."

Marcus nodded.

The ScholarForge terminal pinged—a faint red exclamation icon at the bottom right. ALERT: External source material not aligned with standardized civic history. Please confirm instructional compliance. Marcus clicked Postpone and turned back to the class.

"Let me ask you something," he said. "If a system breaks your legs, hands you a cane, and tells you to be grateful—what do you call that?"

Mari spoke up. "Gaslighting." "Exactly. And when it tells you not to talk about how it happened?" Elijah raised his hand. "Censorship." Marcus smiled. "Now you're thinking like scholars."

The discussion turned next to language. Marcus wrote the word de facto on the board.

"De facto means 'by fact'—as if segregation just happened by accident. That's the term they use when they don't want to admit guilt. But The Color of Law proves it was de jure—by law. Backed by the federal government. Enforced through zoning, lending, and silence." A girl in the back, Sofia, murmured, "So... my grandma's neighborhood was redlined too. I looked it up. My family's still there. My uncle still can't get a loan." Marcus let her words settle. "That's not coincidence. That's policy echoing through generations." Before they dismissed, he handed each student a printed page with three quotes: "You can't understand present inequality unless you know the architecture of the past." —Richard Rothstein

"The struggle of memory against forgetting is a form of resistance." —Milan Kundera

"Our true history lives in our books, our minds, and the lessons we teach each other when no one else is watching." —Marcus Baker

Each student tucked the sheet into their notebook.

Mari folded hers with care and whispered, "I'm showing this to my mom." Back at Graham Manor that evening, Langston reviewed the surveillance logs. "Marcus tripped three ScholarForge flags," Monroe reported. "One for redlining content. One for Rothstein. One for nonstandard narrative emphasis."

Langston looked up from his notes.

"And student engagement?"

"Highest it's been since the portal opened."

Langston allowed himself a small smile. He walked to the window, salt-and-pepper beard catching the warm lamplight. "Let the system log the alerts. We're not here to soothe algorithms. We're here to wake up minds." He turned.

"Prepare the next module."

Chapter 17: The Sacred Classroom

From Langston's Journal: "There must always remain in every life some place for the singing of angels." —Howard Thurman

The sanctuary of Zion Hill AME was quiet, save for the creak of the century-old pews and the gentle hum of stained-glass catching afternoon light.

Langston Graham stood behind the pulpit. He was not there to preach—though the ancestors in the front row portraits might've insisted otherwise. He was there to teach. To remember. To plant. The program had been billed as a "Community Reflection on Truth and Education," but everyone in the room knew it was more than that. They came because truth was under siege. And because, for generations, this space had been the only safe place to learn it. Behind Langston, the altar remained undisturbed. A single Bible lay open to Proverbs. But beneath it, tucked into the lectern, was a worn copy of an early sermon collection by Alexander Crummell.

Langston tapped it gently.

"Before we had classrooms," he began, "We had churches."

He paused to let the memory breathe. "It was in spaces like this—on wooden benches, by lamplight, between sermons—that Black education was born. Not just learning to read the Bible, but to read the world. To ask: Why were we denied this knowledge? And who profits from our ignorance?"

A murmur moved through the crowd. "Alexander Crummell, writing in 1880, called education 'the redemption of the race.' He believed it was the church's duty to teach—not just faith, but freedom. And what did he mean by that?" Langston held up the book. "He meant that literacy without liberation is a half-built bridge." He moved from the lectern and stood closer to the congregation, hands clasped. "In the fields, they whispered lessons. In hush arbors, they learned letters. In praise houses, they decoded survival. That was the Black church—the first campus of our people. And no school board, no government, and no surveillance portal can take that origin from us." In the back, Monroe stood watching. Her presence, as always, was poised and quiet. She wasn't taking notes. She didn't need to. Every word would stay with her. Langston turned to a page marked with a cloth ribbon. "Howard Thurman—pastor, mystic, scholar—once said: 'There is something in every one of you that waits and listens for the sound of the genuine in yourself… It is the only true guide you will ever have.'" He looked out over the sanctuary. "So, the question isn't just what we're teaching. It's who we're allowing to teach us how to see ourselves." He scanned the front row—

elders, teachers, young parents with children in their laps.

"You cannot be guided by the genuine if you've been handed a false story of your past."

A soft hum of agreement moved through the crowd.

"They tell us diversity is dangerous. That equity is an affront to justice. But hear me clearly: it is the injustice that made DEI necessary. Equity isn't a disruption. It's a form of repair."

He stepped forward.

"And that's what Crummell meant when he said education is armor. Because when you walk into a room armed with truth, you don't need to shout. You don't need permission. You just stand." He reached for a small stack of printed cards Monroe had placed at the edge of the altar. He held one up.

"Each of you will leave with one of these. On it is a quote from Thurman: 'Don't ask what the world needs. Ask what makes you come alive… Because what the world needs is people who have come alive.'"

Langston placed the card down and looked out again.

"You are not here to memorize facts. You are here to remember yourselves. The sacred classroom begins here. And it never ends."

A long silence followed—not empty, but full.

Then an elder in the back—Deacon Isaiah—stood and raised his hand. "Dr.

Graham," he said, "is there a way we can make this permanent? Can our church be a site of study again?"

Langston nodded. "Yes. It already is." He stepped down from the pulpit. "I will donate the curriculum. We'll begin with Crummell and Thurman. And we will teach truth. Regardless of what the system allows."

The church, in that moment, felt like something more than holy ground. It felt like homework.

That night, back at Graham Manor, Langston sat with Marcus in the west study.

"The church wants to begin a Freedom Learning Circle," Langston said. Marcus looked up from his journal. "And they want you to lead it?" Langston shook his head. "They want us to lead it." Marcus nodded, then opened his Moroccan notebook.

On the next page, he wrote:

The classroom has no walls.

The pulpit is a portal.

And truth is the curriculum that survived the fire. He looked up.

"I'm ready."

Langston smiled. "Then we begin at Zion Hill."

Outside, the wind picked up. But inside the manor, the lamps burned long into the night.

Chapter 18: Default Protocol

Langston raised an eyebrow, the congressional light above him casting long shadows across the oak-paneled hearing room.

"Of course they do," he said quietly, but firmly. "A system this bloated doesn't collapse without squealing. Massive student loan defaults feed their engine. Debt collectors, private servicers, third-party guarantors—every layer is owned by someone higher up the food chain. It's not just mismanagement. It's design." A few pens stilled. Cameras blinked. "Student loan default isn't failure," Langston continued, leaning into the mic. "It's business. The longer people can't pay, the more they owe. The more they owe, the more Wall Street harvests— through interest, collections, and buyout contracts. A nation of debtors is a nation too tired to rebel."

There was a rustle behind him as Monroe adjusted her stance, hand never far from the sealed folder of classified audits they'd leaked weeks earlier.

Representative Warren opened a leather folder of his own and glanced at Langston over wire-rimmed glasses. "The House Minority Caucus wants to draft a resolution. Symbolic, maybe. But we'd cite your testimony, use it to reignite debate over student debt enforcement and agency overreach." He paused.

"We'd need you to testify—formally. On record."

Langston didn't flinch. His fingers laced together like a clasped verdict. Warren exhaled. "You'll be painting a bullseye on your back. Bigger than before."

Langston nodded slowly. "Then aim high. I have no interest in survival. Only legacy."

Warren closed the folder. "There'll be a hearing in three weeks. We'll start there. My office will provide temporary legal shielding. It won't stop everything, but it'll slow them down."

Langston stood, gaze already beyond the room. "They can subpoena my silence, but not my memory."

Chapter 19 – By Design: When Debt Becomes Doctrine

Langston Graham stood before a blackboard filled with numbers, charts, and names that traced not just policies— but patterns. Marcus had pinned a headline on the wall behind him: *"Wall Street's* Quiet *Harvest: The Business of Student Debt."*

"Let me be clear," Langston began, his voice low and measured. "This isn't failure. This is functioning as intended."

He pointed to a chart showing $1.7 trillion in student loan debt. "Forty-five million Americans. That's not an accident. That's a market."

Behind him, Monroe paced slowly, reading aloud the figures taped to the wall. "Black students borrow more. Black graduates owe more. Black repayment rates lag behind. Black borrowers see none of the promised return."

Langston turned. "That's because the return isn't for them. It's for Wall Street."

He walked to the center of the room and pulled down a projection—an organizational chart showing the Department of Education's relationship with private loan servicers and guaranty agencies. "These aren't student loans. These are asset-backed securities.

Bundled, traded, leveraged."
Monroe added, "And default doesn't cancel the transaction—it inflates it."

They stared at the reality: every missed payment, every delay, every deferment—it didn't represent loss to the system. It was profit. Debt collectors tacked on fees. Servicers padded their margins. Investors earned interest. And if the borrower defaulted? Wage garnishment. Tax refund seizures. Social Security offsets.

Marcus read from his notes: "Twelve years after graduation, the average Black borrower owes more than they originally borrowed. Meanwhile, the average White borrower has paid down 35%."

Langston nodded grimly. "Because wealth protects you from interest. Racism doesn't."

They paused on a quote from Jalil Mustaffa's *Jim Crow Debt* report:

"Debt is not neutral. It is racialized. And its consequences are compounded by the same forces that built redlining, mass incarceration, and segregated schools."

Langston leaned on the table, fingers clasped. "This is not about education. This is about extraction. About stripping the economic potential from Black futures before they bloom. And funneling it— every dollar of it—upward."

He clicked to a slide showing Nelnet, Navient, and other student loan servicers. "These companies are not educational institutions. They are debt merchants. They buy, sell, and trade obligation like stock."

Monroe added, "And they do it knowing that Black borrowers—disproportionately first-generation, with less inherited wealth—are the most vulnerable. They *engineer* these outcomes. Because pain is profitable."

Langston's voice dropped. "You want to know what systemic racism looks like in the 21st century? It's a six-figure debt, a garnished paycheck, a degree that can't pay for itself, and a credit report that locks you out of homeownership."

He paused, letting the silence settle. Then he picked up a file: Nina's story.

"$900 a month in payments. Earnings as low as $700. And when she asked what would happen if she died, they told her they'd come after her father."

He closed the file.

"This is not just immoral. It is monstrous."

Marcus added, "And it's killing people. Sixty-four percent of Black borrowers report mental health issues directly linked to student debt. Depression. Anxiety. Suicidal thoughts. The government mandates repayment—but not relief." Langston drew a line across the whiteboard. One side said **Wall Street**. The other: **Main Street**.

"This line," he said, "isn't just economic.

It's racial. It's generational. It's historic."

He circled the numbers.

"$65,135 – median income for Black degree holders."
"$77,162 – median for White degree holders."
"$24,100 – median Black household wealth."
"$188,200 – median White household wealth."

"These aren't just gaps. They're gulfs. And they are the design specifications of an economy built on exclusion."

Langston turned back to the group.

"Wage gaps. Wealth gaps. Debt gaps. The trifecta of modern control. This is how you keep people chasing freedom but never finding it. You promise a way out through education—then turn that promise into a contract of servitude."

Monroe leaned against the table, jaw clenched. "And still, we tell our children to go to college. Still, we tell them it's their only way up."

"Because what else can we say?"
Langston replied. "That the dream is
rigged? That their ambition is a revenue
stream for investors who will never know
their names?"

Marcus whispered, "Then we have to say
something else. We have to build
something else."

Langston nodded. He pulled out the next
unit plan for ScholarForge: **"Debt by
Design: Structural Racism, Capital
Markets, and the Illusion of
Meritocracy."**

The first case study? Maya.

*"From day one, the chips were stacked
against the Black/African American
community... because Black people
disproportionately do not have the
access."*

Langston wrote her name in bold on the
chalkboard.

"This is the curriculum of resistance," he
said. "This is how we fight back—not with
slogans, but with structure. With evidence.
With education that unmasks the lie."

Monroe looked up. "And what do we call
this chapter?"

Langston looked back at the whiteboard, then at the chart dividing Wall Street and Main Street.

"By Design," he said. "Because that's exactly what it is."

Chapter 20: The Ones Who Played by the Rules

The hall was empty except for the soft hum of the old projector and the scent of chalk that still clung to the air like memory. Dr. Langston Graham stood in front of the screen, arms folded, eyes scanning a photo that filled the frame: a high school graduation class from 1993. Rows of faces full of promise. Caps cocked. Tassels mid-swing. Names printed on the back in faded Sharpie. "These are the ones who played by the rules," he said. Marcus sat in the third row, elbows on the desk, eyes locked in. "What happened to them?"
Langston didn't answer right away. He let the silence thicken like old blood. "They were told," he finally said, "that education was the ladder. That if they stayed off the streets, avoided the pull of crack and corner hustles, if they did the work, earned the grades, they could rise. They were told that Pell Grants and Stafford Loans were steppingstones. That debt was a temporary cost for a permanent gain." He clicked forward. The next slide showed the same faces years later—tired now. A collage of social media photos, job ID badges, mugshots. One wore a nursing uniform. One had a Department of Corrections badge. Another was holding a sign at a protest: $147K and Still Paying.

Langston tapped the screen. "They took out the loans at 17, 18, 19 years old—barely old enough to rent a car. They signed on dotted lines after guidance counselors told them it was normal. Safe. Smart. They avoided the streets and wound up on a different leash." The rear door eased open, and Monroe stepped in, silent as always, her blazer folded over one arm, her presence calm but vigilant. She'd seen this lesson before—but even she didn't interrupt.

Langston paced.

"While crack was flooding communities, decimating families, and justifying mass incarceration, these young people chose the classroom over the block. They turned in papers while their friends turned to survival. They did what the nation said was right." He stopped.

"And they were punished for it." Marcus looked down. "They trusted the system."

Langston nodded. "And now they teach in it. They clean it. They try to fix it from the inside, drowning in debt that keeps growing. Because you see—it's not just a loan. It's a sentence." He lowered his voice.

"Here's what they won't say out loud: the same corporations and business interests who profit from loan default today—those same financial titans were the ones begging for help in 2008. When the housing bubble burst and the market collapsed, they said they were too big to fail. The government poured billions into their accounts without blinking. No paperwork. No delay. No shame." He turned back toward the class photo. "But now that it's the individual crying out— the teacher, the nurse, the social worker who took out loans at 18 trying to climb out of poverty—the response is different. The government hesitates. Congress fumbles. The answer is no. They say, 'personal responsibility.' They say, 'You signed the loan.' They say, 'Figure it out.'" Langston's voice hardened.

"So let me get this straight: When Wall Street's house was burning, we called it an emergency. But when Main Street's future is on fire, we call it a moral failing." He clicked again.

This slide was blank.

"Nothing teaches better than example," Langston said. "And when the example is: 'get educated, stay broke,' then don't be surprised when children stop dreaming. When boys with gifted hands choose hustle over homework. When girls with top grades choose TikTok over tuition." He turned off the projector.

"So yes, Wall Street benefits from default. But the cost? The cost is trust. Hope. Legacy. We are burning the ladder we once begged them to climb." Marcus raised a hand. "Is that the plan?" Langston paused. His voice came quieter than expected.

"If it is… then it's not just debt collection. It's cultural erasure. A silent war on every child who dares to believe that learning is still a way out."

He walked past the front row, hands in his pockets.

"History calls that forced servitude. Modernity just calls it interest."

Monroe's Journal — Entry 47
Location: Graham Manor, Lower Study
Date: April 11, 2025
Time: 11:14 PM
Today, I watched him stand in front of ghosts.

Rows of empty desks. Faces that no longer needed the projector to be remembered. He called them the ones who played by the rules. I could feel the weight in his voice. Not anger, not even grief—something worse. Betrayal.

He showed their smiles first. Senior portraits with ambition still alive in their posture. Some of them could have been me. Could have been him. Then came the slide of what happened after: the fatigue of survival. The quiet war waged through interest rates, garnishments, deferments, and dreams too expensive to keep. It's one thing to owe a bank. It's another thing to owe a country that promised you a future.

I kept to the back of the room, as I often do. My presence is clearest when I don't speak.

But when he said, "They turned in papers while their friends turned to survival," I thought about the boys on my block. I remember Raymond—gifted programming computers, never made it past 10th grade.

I remember Dena—pregnant by 16, dead by 24. And I remember myself, watching them fall one by one, thinking maybe—just maybe—I had escaped. But tonight reminded me: some cages are just invisible.

Langston called it cultural erasure. He's right. They're not burning schools. They're burning faith in them. Every teacher who works two jobs. Every grad student eating instant noodles under mountains of debt. Every little cousin asking if college is "still worth it." We know what this is. We just didn't expect it to come with handshakes and federal logos.

They'll come for him. Maybe for me too. But I've made peace with that. We're not in this for safety.

We're in this for memory. And for those who never got to write their own.

—Monroe.

Chapter 21: The Price of Liberation

The lights in the Wellspring briefing room dimmed to near darkness. Rows of students and professors leaned in, the glow of a single projector casting long shadows across their faces.

On the screen stood three simple bars. No flames, no slogans. Just numbers: $9,400 – One-time cost per taxpayer for full student loan forgiveness $940/year – Spread over 10 years $600/year or less – Under progressive taxation Langston Graham stepped forward, wearing a deep navy wool blazer over a subtle glen plaid shirt—no tie, sleeves casually pushed up to his elbows. He didn't look like a mogul tonight. He looked like a professor in war mode. "You ever notice," he said, "that the word 'bailout' only becomes a dirty word when
it's for the poor?"

A nervous chuckle fluttered from the back. Langston ignored it.

"They bailed out Wall Street in 2008. They bailed out airlines. They bailed out oil. Nobody asked if those people 'deserved it.' But when we talk about canceling the chains that keep teachers, social workers, and first-generation students in debt until death—suddenly we become moral accountants?" He walked slowly past the projector screen. "I've run the numbers. I've built models that predict learning outcomes, political trends, even currency shifts. But nothing has been more carefully designed than the illusion that student debt is just financial issue. It's not."

He clicked a remote.

A second slide replaced the chart—an image of an elderly Black woman, face weary but proud, her Social Security check showing a $217 monthly deduction for a loan she took out in 1982 to attend a now-defunct trade school.

Langston pointed.

"She had a stroke in 2021. Lives alone in Mississippi. Her heat was shut off in January. Why? Because she borrowed $4,000 to learn bookkeeping in the Reagan era. That school closed. The degree is worthless. But the interest? Eternal." He paused.

"This isn't about fairness. This is about obedience."

A few students shifted in their seats, the discomfort sharp now. Langston turned, voice rising. "A nation that can erase the debts of slaveholders in 1862 should be able to forgive the debt of those trying to become teachers
in 2025."

The room went still.

"I carry the blood," he said, eyes scanning the crowd, "of those who built this nation with their hands—and those who stole it with their pens. Both truths live in me." A ripple of recognition passed through

Marcus as he wrote those words down in his journal.

Langston's voice dropped low.

"You know what we never talk about? That this debt—this massive number on paper—isn't even real money. It's projected repayment. It's the idea of money. But to the debtor, it's very real. It's the house you didn't buy. The job you couldn't leave. The medication you skipped. The baby you delayed. The freedom you deferred." Another chart. This one showed default rates by ZIP code.

"Student loan default isn't randomly distributed," Langston explained. "It's mapped. It's targeted. The ZIP codes with the highest rates? Black, brown, rural, and poor. We used to call that redlining." He tapped the board.

"We still should."

Then a final image: Frederick Douglass holding a worn book, eyes intense. Over it, the quote:

"Power concedes nothing without a demand."

"I understand the argument about fairness," Dr. Graham began, his voice calm but resolute as he stood before the auditorium. "I've heard the frustration from those who worked multiple jobs to pay off every dollar, those who sacrificed to meet their obligations. That perspective deserves acknowledgment. But fairness, by itself, can't be our only measure—not when the system was never fair to begin with. If we're honest, we must admit that student debt was designed to trap, not to uplift—especially for the poor, the first generation, and the descendants of those who were locked out of wealth by law and custom. To call repayment 'fair' while ignoring how the system disproportionately punished some and privileged others is to mistake compliance for justice."

Dr. Graham stepped closer, lowering his tone with conviction. "Justice requires us to do more than repeat the rules; it calls us to examine how those rules were written, and who they were written for. When we cancel student debt, we're not erasing responsibility—we're interrupting a cycle of generational punishment. We're saying that a teacher in Mississippi, a nurse in Detroit, or a coder from a Baltimore charter school deserves the chance to build without a financial chain around their ankle. Justice isn't always symmetrical— but it is always intentional. If we truly want a society where education is a path to freedom, not bondage, then cancellation is not charity. It's correction."

Langston faced the room once more. "Forgiveness isn't a handout. It's a reset. It's not about erasing effort—it's about erasing a rigged game." He let that sink in. "Liberation isn't free. But the price shouldn't be lifelong bondage." He closed the laptop. The screen went dark.

One student, a first-year college student from South Carolina, raised her hand and asked, "Dr. Graham… do you think debt cancellation will ever happen?" Langston exhaled. "I think it has to. Not just for justice—but for survival." Marcus looked up.

And for the first time, he understood why ScholarForge wasn't just an AI company.

It was a war memorial.

And this—this was a battlefield.

Chapter 22: The Room Without Echoes

There was a door within the west library no one else knew existed—not even Monroe, whose precision and perception rivaled any intelligence analyst. Tucked behind a false panel of law journals and obscure theology tomes, it opened only by pressing the spine of a weathered leatherbound volume of Cicero's *De Officiis*.

Beyond that narrow passage lay a room no larger than a monk's cell but built with the deliberateness of a vault. The walls were padded, lined in velvet-damask and reinforced with soundproofing insulation so dense not even vibration could escape. No light bled in. No sound leaked out.

This was Langston Graham's sanctum.

Inside, a single worn leather wing chair sat like a throne. The corners bore the deep creases of thought—creases etched by years of silent rebellion, intellectual rigor, and the discipline of stillness. A Persian rug lay beneath it, its colors muted by time and dust, though Langston never let the space grow too unkempt. On the far wall, a miniature refrigerator hummed faintly— a quiet sentinel for the six bottles of mineral water he kept chilled and untouched until the end of each meditation.

But the silence, paradoxically, was filled. The moment he closed the door and reclined into the chair, Langston clicked the remote on a concealed speaker embedded above. Instantly, the searing intro of *Gimme Shelter* by The Rolling Stones exploded into the chamber like a riot.

Outside, the house remained undisturbed. Not even the dust on the library shelves would have stirred.

Inside, Langston Graham closed his eyes.

The music was not a distraction. It was a crucible.

Years ago—when he was just a wiry seventeen-year-old in Trenton, full of grief, brilliance, and rage—he had trained in Tang Soo Do under Master Chambers, a quiet war veteran with a steel spine and mahogany knuckles. Master Chambers once stood motionless in the middle of a circle of sparring students, his eyes closed, as chaos erupted around him.

When Langston asked how he could ignore the noise, Master Chambers had said only one thing:

"Focus is not quiet. It is command. If you can master your mind in noise, silence becomes your slave."

It became a mantra for Langston. And in the years since, he had tested it. In courtroom debates. In classrooms under threat. In media interviews with hostile pundits. But nowhere did he test it more rigorously than here, in the room without echoes.

As the guitar riffs surged and Mick Jagger's voice howled about war, children, and madness, Langston sank deeper into his breath.

Inhale: the legacy of resilience. Hold: the memory of injustice. Exhale: the need to carry everything at once.

Each breath was a negotiation with the past. A cleansing of the daily battles that clawed at his psyche. Here, no one could interrupt. Not ScholarForge. Not Monroe. Not even the guilt he carried for not being able to save everyone.

Time lost its grip in that space. Sometimes twenty minutes passed. Sometimes two hours.

When the final bars of the song faded, Langston opened his eyes—not startled, not stirred, but sharpened. He rose, retrieved a bottle of water, and took a single sip. Cold clarity slid down his throat.

Before he opened the hidden door again, he whispered aloud a single word.

"Chambers."
A nod to the man who taught him how to still the storm by stepping directly into it. Then, as silently as he had arrived, Dr. Langston Elkanah Graham disappeared back into the world.

Chapter 23: Default by Design

Langston Graham descended into the Wellspring archives like a man searching not just for history—but for a body. The metal drawer screeched open, and the documents inside breathed dust into the air like ashes.

He found the file. Thin, weathered, but deadly.

Label: Georgia State Penitentiary – 1878–1912

Inside: arrest reports, labor contracts, and medical records that read more like eulogies than files.

He flipped through pages.

"Isaiah Brown, Negro male, 19. Offense: Vagrancy. Sentence: 10 years hard labor. Leased to Catoosa Iron Works. Died, Year 2. Cause: Heatstroke. No burial noted."

Langston didn't speak. He simply pressed the folder shut, holding it like a truth no one had asked to hear, but everyone needed.

He brought it upstairs. That afternoon, the classroom lights dimmed, and the projector screen glowed with a black and-white photograph: men in striped uniforms, shackled in rows, shoveling gravel into carts under armed guard.

The class went still.

"This is not a prison photo," Langston began. "This is a business record." Click.

A map of the South filled the screen.

Railroads. Mines. Cotton fields. All color-coded by convict lease routes. "After the 13th Amendment abolished slavery," Langston continued, "the United States discovered a loophole: except as punishment for a crime. So, they created crimes." Click.
Arrest charges scrolled down the screen:
Loitering
Vagrancy
Talking back
Not carrying work papers
Insulting a white woman
"These weren't crimes," Langston said. "They were traps." Click.
A contract appeared:
State of Alabama leases 125 convicts to Birmingham Steel Company for $9 per head per month.
Langston's voice dropped. "They didn't need whips anymore. They had judges. They didn't need slave patrols. They had sheriffs."
He let the class sit with that.
"But let's not get sentimental," he said. "They weren't just after labor. They were after control. If you could keep a people in chains—even invisible ones—you didn't have to fear their freedom." Click. The next slide jarred them. A modern image: a line of Black and brown students outside a financial aid office. FAFSA packets. Blank stares. Suitcases of expectation.
"This is how it looks today," Langston said.
Click.

A chart filled the screen: Average
Black borrower: $52,000 in student
loan debt
Default rate: 3x higher than white peers 20
years later: most still owe more than the
original balance
Langston moved to the center of the room.
"You weren't arrested this time," he said.
"You were recruited. Sold a dream. Given
a pen instead of a chain. But the outcome
is eerily familiar."
He let the screen go dark and spoke
without the slideshow.
"Student loans are not just about money.
They are about containment. They make
sure you stay obedient. That you don't
build too much wealth, question too
loudly, or leave your job when it insults
your spirit."
He raised a hand slowly, like he was
lifting a truth from the floor. "Default is
not an accident," he said. "It is a
design."
He turned to the students. "You will hear
that you must be more responsible. That
you chose this debt. That you should just
work harder. But let me remind you—
Isaiah Brown didn't choose the Iron
Works. He was sentenced." He raised the
file in his hand. "This right here is not
history. It's prophecy. And we're still
living in its shadow."
A hand went up. Jaya, a first-generation
college student from Houston. "Dr.
Graham… are you saying education isn't
worth it?"

Langston's face softened, but his eyes stayed sharp.

"No," he said. "I am saying the opposite. Education is everything. But we must stop confusing education with the systems that sell it."

He paced.

"Education is sacred. It's how I built ScholarForge. It's how you survive. It's the weapon our ancestors were beaten for holding. But we must reclaim it—not as a market, but as an inheritance." He paused by the window. Outside, a group of middle schoolers toured the Wellspring grounds.

"Education is not the enemy," he said. "Debt is. Predatory systems are. False promises are." He turned back to the room. "We must teach ourselves and our descendants the truth. About history. About money. About power. Because if they control the curriculum, they control the future."

Another hand, Marcus this time. "Then how do we break the cycle?" Langston looked at him—not as a student, but as a future builder.

"We forge," he said. "In secret if we must. In code. In memory. In defiance." He placed the folder down gently.

"ScholarForge is not just a company. It's a message. We remember. We resist. We rebuild." Click.

A Frederick Douglass quote filled the screen:

"It is easier to build strong children than to repair broken men."

Langston stepped away.

"That's why we educate. That's why we fight."

He paused, then added—voice low but unflinching:

"But let me be clear. Not everyone receives the same justice, even under the same Constitution." He clicked once more.

Two photos appeared side by side: one of a northern detention center under court threat of federal takeover, the other a southern prison riddled with deaths, lawsuits, and federal investigations—yet still under local control.

"No mandate came for this one," he said, pointing to the southern photo. "Just headlines. Just suggestions." He looked across the room. "Where you are determines what kind of justice you get. Not because the law changes—but because the will to enforce it does."

Langston folded his hands behind his back.

"This country claims to run on mandates," he said. "But too often, it runs on mercy… doled out by region, race, and reputation."

He left the photos up. The class didn't move. No one took notes. They just sat in the silence—where truth had landed and still burned.

The ScholarForge Manifesto

A Declaration for the Free Mind and the
Bound Soul
*"If they won't let us through the gates, we
build tunnels."*
— Dr. Langston Elkanah Graham
We are the inheritors of stolen labor and
stolen futures.
They told us education was the key but
handed us shackles instead. They built
cathedrals of knowledge and guarded them
with gatekeepers, algorithms, and interest
rates.
We reject the myth of meritocracy. We
know the system was not broken. It was
built to function this way—to extract
obedience, to normalize struggle, and to
reward silence.
We refuse to default on our dignity. To
default is to surrender to a system
designed to keep us in permanent
payment. ScholarForge declares we are
not your debtors—we are your designers.
Our tools are memory and code. We
build underground networks of
knowledge.
We encrypt our stories in the language of
data, faith, and resistance. We believe
learning is a sacred inheritance—not a
commodity.
We believe that knowledge is not neutral.

It can either liberate or reinforce the cage.
ScholarForge chooses liberation. We will
not wait for forgiveness. We will
engineer our freedom.
Our tuition was already paid by those who
bled, marched, taught in basements, and
whispered truth in cotton fields and union
halls.
This is not charity. This is restoration.
We will teach. We will resist. We will
remember.
And when the next generation asks
who freed them, they will not point to
presidents or banks. They will point to
us. ScholarForge is not a brand. It is a
rebellion.

Chapter 24: The Bitter Taste of Wisdom

Marcus had never lived in a place so quiet.
The creak of old wood, the whisper of
central air through antique vents, and the
occasional rustle of wind in the ivy outside
were now the sounds that filled his days.
Langston had cleared out one of the guest
rooms on the second floor of Graham
Manor after Aunt Pam passed, claiming
that young minds needed grounding more
than independence. The room had crown
molding, bookshelves already stocked
with Baldwin, Butler, Baldwin again, and
the faint scent of cedar embedded in the
walls. But for Marcus, it was still strange
to wake up without the TV buzzing in the
background or Aunt Pam's radio playing
gospel too loud for 6 a.m. He missed her
something terrible. Langston rarely spoke
of grief in direct terms. Instead, he handed
Marcus articles on stoicism or pulled
books from shelves that were
"coincidentally" about fathers, mentors, or
rites of passage. Tonight, though, he didn't
give a book. He handed him a bowl.
Marcus frowned. "What is this?" Langston
sat across from him at the kitchen table,
the overhead light casting warm shadows
across the long oak surface. "Pot likker."
Marcus stared at the broth. It was
greenish, a little oily on top, with flecks of
collard leaves and a chunk or two of
smoked turkey. "You made this?"
Langston nodded, pulling his own bowl
closer. "It's how I was raised. Collards

cooked down slow—with garlic, onion, a little vinegar, and something smoked. What's left in the pot after the greens are gone... that's the likker. That's where the soul is."

Marcus picked up his spoon like it might bite him. He took a tentative sip—and winced. "It's bitter."

Langston chuckled. "I know."

"You eat this on purpose?" "Yes. I sip it like soup. But when I was your age—" He paused, swirling the liquid in his bowl. "I couldn't stand the stuff. Thought my grandmother was trying to punish me."

Marcus leaned back, spoon still hovering. "She made you drink it?" Langston's eyes went distant for a moment.

Trenton, 1981

It was January in Trenton, and the draft coming through the cracked windows bit harder than any lesson Langston learned in school that day. He sat at the tiny kitchen table, coat still on, staring down at a chipped mug filled with what looked like murky pond water.

"Drink it," Grandma Patty said, turning back to the stove.

Langston sniffed it. "Smells like feet."

"You better hush that foolishness," she said without turning. *"That right there is pot likker. That's medicine. That's memory."*

Langston scrunched his nose. "But it's just the leftover water."

Patty turned, a wooden spoon in one hand and a Bible in the other. *"It's what the enslaved used to drink after they cooked greens for the master's table. They weren't allowed to eat the greens, baby— just the water left behind. But that water held the iron, the calcium, the vitamins, the flavor. Everything good the plant gave up."* She pulled out a chair across from him, easing into it slowly. *"That's how we survived. Sippin' what was left. Making medicine out of scraps. You think this is about taste?"*
Langston said nothing.
She leaned in close, her eyes fierce. *"One day you'll be full grown, talkin' all that educated talk, and forget what got you here. But not today. Today you gon' sip."*
He obeyed—grudgingly. The bitterness made him twitch. But it stayed with him.

Back in the Present
Marcus watched him for a moment, then took another sip. Still bitter—but not as bad.
"You're saying this is like... survival food?"
Langston nodded. "It's a metaphor, too. This world will feed you scraps. Sometimes you gotta learn to sip slow. To draw strength from what others, throw away."
Marcus tilted his head. "Like ScholarForge."
"Exactly," Langston said. "Like you. People wrote you off. You're the pot

likker, Marcus. You carry the nutrients of a thousand discarded stories."

For a moment, Marcus didn't speak. Then he finished the rest of his bowl in silence. When he looked up, there was no longer distance in Langston's gaze—only recognition. The kind that passes from one survivor to another. The kind that begins the long, unspoken covenant of men who raise up legacy not through blood, but through belief.

Langston stood. "Tomorrow, I want you in the study. I'll be reviewing some old ScholarForge blueprints. Time you learned how this house was really built." Marcus nodded. "Can I bring the rest of this?" Langston smiled. "Now you're learning."

Chapter 25: Guardrails

The auditorium lights dimmed as the moderator introduced him. "Dr. Langston Elkanah Graham— educator, author, and founder of ScholarForge—has joined us tonight not just to talk about education, but about the erosion of the very ideals meant to hold this republic together." Langston adjusted his gold-rimmed glasses. The spotlight warmed his brow as he stepped to the podium. His camel hair blazer hung effortlessly from his shoulders, and the worn leather journal Monroe had given him was tucked in the crook of his arm. He did not read from it. He didn't need to. He leaned into the mic, his voice measured, deliberate.
"Imagine a winding road at night.
No streetlights.
A sheer drop on one side.
And someone—somewhere—decides to take down the guardrails." A murmur rippled through the crowd. "Not because the road has changed. Not because the danger has passed. But because they believe you shouldn't need them." He
paused.
"That's what it feels like. Watching the dismantling of DEI programs. The rollback of Civil Rights protections. The erasure of race-conscious policies.
It feels like watching someone remove the guardrails—not from a country—but from you. From your children. From the future."

His voice sharpened, not angry—but unsparing.

"Let's be clear: These were never handouts.

They were correctives.

Not advantages.

Guardrails.

To prevent the system from tipping into the same ravine of exclusion and economic violence it has always known."

He clicked a slide behind him. A photo of a segregated school dated 1957. Another: a redlined neighborhood map. Then another: a recent news headline, "University Ends Diversity Hiring Program."

"They say they're restoring fairness. That everyone should 'compete equally.' But I ask: when did the competition ever begin on equal terms?"

He stepped from behind the podium now, speaking directly, without ornament.

"Let's talk about their guardrails. Legacy admissions.

Tax-exempt generational wealth.

Real estate loopholes.

Political networks forged in prep schools and private clubs.

And nobody calls those handouts.

They call them 'tradition.'

Or 'merit.'

Or 'policy.'"

A silence filled the space like reverence— or revelation.

"So let me flip the script.

What if we removed their guardrails?

No legacy preferences.

No insider lobbying.
No subsidies for oil barons or billion
dollar banks.
Would they call that justice—or an attack
on the American Dream?" A single nod
from the back row grew into a tide of
heads slowly agreeing. "When you remove
guardrails from our lane, it's called
fairness. When you threaten theirs, it's
called chaos.
That's not equity.
That's hypocrisy with a press pass."
Langston let the words settle. "You
see, justice has never been the
absence of structure.
Justice is the presence of moral design.
Guardrails are not barriers.
They are boundaries against backsliding.
They keep us from returning to the ditch
we once called Jim Crow, or the canyon
we labeled 'colorblind' while watching
communities drown."
He returned to the podium, placed both
hands on its edge.
"I'm not here to defend programs.
I'm here to defend people.
To say that the road to equity is dangerous
enough.
And we need all the protection we can
get."
"So, the next time someone says, 'Tear it
all down. Let people stand on their own,'
ask them—
'Will you dismantle your own guardrails
first?'"
The crowd stood before he was finished.

He didn't ask for applause. He
asked for accountability. And
for a road that didn't just lead somewhere
better—
—but didn't throw people off the edge
along the way.

Chapter 26: Ashes on the Page

Langston stared at the screen longer than he needed to.

The headline sat like a bruise on the morning newsfeed:

"Faith Leaders Condemn Hate Crime After

100 Library Books on Black, Jewish, and LGBTQ+ History Burned in Iowa." It wasn't the first time he had seen such a story.

But this time, it hit different. There, in grainy video footage leaked from a white supremacist Telegram group, someone was tossing books—his people's stories—into a fire. Charred spines curled under the heat. Titles like Black Radical, Fighting Auschwitz, The ABCs of Queer History flickered briefly before disintegrating into smoke. Someone off camera laughed.

"We are cleansing our libraries of degenerate filth," the caption read. Langston's jaw tightened. Not in shock. In confirmation.

He turned to Monroe, who had been silently watching from the doorway. Her expression was cold, professional, but Langston knew her well enough to hear the fury humming behind it. "They always come for the books first," she said quietly.

He nodded. "Then the people." She stepped into the room and laid a printed report on his desk—testimony from faith leaders in Ohio, members of a grassroots group called the Interfaith Group Against Hate. The leader, Rev. Raheem Wallace, had said what Langston was already thinking: "I'm shocked, but not surprised."

The act hadn't been random. It had been deliberate. Coordinated. The man had checked out the books legally from the Cuyahouthga County Public Library, filmed himself burning them, and then uploaded the footage for white supremacists to cheer. Stickers with slogans like "White Lives Matter" and "Everything Beautiful is White" had been found throughout Ohio in recent months. This was no isolated act of rage—it was ideology with gasoline. Langston stood and walked to the wide window that overlooked the south lawn of Graham Manor. The mist had not yet lifted. He reached for his journal. "Ashes on the page become embers in the bloodstream of a nation too scared to remember," he wrote.

Then he paused.

"This is why ScholarForge was born," he said aloud.

"Not just to educate. But to defend memory. To keep the ink wet when they try to burn the parchment." He recalled what his grandmother, Patty, once told him when he was just a boy: *Baby, the truth got enemies. It always has. Don't you let 'em starve it or silence it.*

Langston moved toward the bookshelf that held some of the very titles now turned to ash in Ohio. He ran his fingers over the spines like a pastor touching relics—text after text written by voices that were never supposed to survive.

He knew the deeper danger wasn't just the act of burning books.

It was the country's growing comfort with the smell of it.

The Beachville police had opened an investigation. Politicians had issued statements. And yet, he knew how these stories usually ended: with distractions, denials, and a slow fade from the public's mind.

But not this time.

Not if he had anything to say about it.

He reached for the intercom on his desk.

"Monroe," he said, "I want a ScholarForge response published within 48 hours. A reading list of the burned titles. A partnership with the Interfaith Group Against Hate. And a national donation campaign to replace every single book tenfold."

"Already in motion," she replied. "The press team has a draft, and we've contacted the library. They're welcoming the support."

Chapter 27: Successors and Scar Tissue

The house was quieter than usual—the kind of silence that makes your thoughts louder.

Langston had brought Marcus into the study after dinner. No lectures, no assignments. Just a gesture toward the wide mahogany table covered in blueprints, hand-drawn schematics, and yellowing receipts. Marcus hovered at the edge, unsure if he should sit or just observe.

Langston tapped one of the blueprints with his silver fountain pen. "This is where it started."

Marcus leaned in. "It says 'Wellspring—Phase I.' What's that?" Langston folded his arms. "Wellspring was the first draft of ScholarForge. A safehouse for minds. Before we had encryption keys or server space, it was just a converted church basement in Newark, New Jersey. Folding chairs. Chalkboard. No funding. Just conviction." Marcus blinked. "All that from a church basement?"

Langston nodded. "That's all I had—and a group of students no one believed in. Starting it... it felt like my black belt test all over again."

Marcus raised an eyebrow. "You did martial arts?"

Langston nodded. "Tang Soo Do. I was fifteen. A Chodan Bo—candidate for black belt. Four of us qualified that year." He paused, a half-smile pulling at one corner of his mouth.

"And we were broke."

Flashback: Trenton to Philadelphia, 1984 – The Road to Black Belt

It was still dark when Master Chambers pulled up in his faded 1974 Ford Comet. The trunk was held shut with bungee cords. The heater barely worked. But none of that mattered.

Langston squeezed into the backseat, wedged between two other boys. The fourth slid in last. All of them wore their doboks under winter coats, belts across their laps like sashes of honor.

"Seatbelts," Chambers snapped.

None of them argued.

They drove the hour to Arch Street in Philadelphia in near silence. Langston kept touching the envelope Grandma Patty had handed him that morning—two hundred dollars in cash. He never knew how she got it. She worked a laundry line job, braided hair on the side. But she pressed it into his hand and said, "Go earn it. Don't waste it."

The gym at Arch Street was already humming with tension. Langston scanned the crowd—dozens of students, instructors, black belts. And in the center of the testing panel sat a long mirror. That mirror made it worse. It didn't just reflect your moves—it reflected your doubts. Langston had been assigned Naihanchi Chodan—the first in a traditional series of black belt Tang Soo Do forms rooted in close-quarters combat. It's a lateral kata, performed in a straight line, with deep horse stances and short, powerful blocks. On the surface, it looked simple. But it was a trap.

Naihanchi Chodan required absolute control. No wasted motion. No drifting focus. The entire kata was built on resisting lateral force—like being squeezed between two collapsing walls. The stance had to be low and rooted. The techniques—blocks, punches, elbows— had to emerge from the hips with force and stillness at once. If you lost your center, you lost everything. Langston hated it. But he respected it. Master Chambers stood to the side, arms crossed. Everyone knew he pulled students from tests if their grades were slipping or if he got wind of misbehavior in school. He had once yanked a student mid-kata for mouthing off to a substitute teacher the week before. No one tested without clean conduct.

Langston stepped to the line.

He bowed.

Breathed.

And began.

His first few movements were solid. But halfway through—during a right inward block with simultaneous elbow strike—his left heel lifted off the ground. Just a sliver. But enough to throw off the center of gravity. Enough for one of the senior masters to make a mark on a clipboard. Langston felt the heat of that mistake rise in his ears.

He thought about the envelope. About Patty Crocker, stiff-knuckled and unbent. About the boys back home, watching, waiting. About Master Chambers, who didn't say much, but whose disappointment could hollow you out like a drum.

Langston locked his heel down like it was nailed to the mat.

And he finished the kata in silence.

Back to the Present

Langston didn't realize his hand was clenched around the table until Marcus spoke.

"You, okay?"

Langston blinked, then exhaled. "Just remembering what it feels like when your whole future depends on not flinching."

He looked at Marcus now, older than Langston had been in that Philadelphia gym, but just as full of quiet doubt.

"You want to know why I'm showing you all this?" Langston said. "Because someone poured into me when they didn't have to. Master Chambers. Grandma Patty. They saw something worth preserving. I'm not just passing you blueprints—I'm handing you a mandate." Marcus looked

down. "You think I can carry all that?"
Langston's eyes didn't waver. "You don't
start with belief. You start with obedience.
With discipline. The belief comes after
you survive the fire."
He turned to the bookshelf and pulled
down an old, soft black belt. The stitching
was nearly gone, the color faded like
charcoal rubbed thin.
"I earned this with a bruised shin, a rolled
ankle, and a kata that nearly broke me.
And $200 my grandma probably didn't
even have."
He handed it to Marcus.
"This isn't just about ScholarForge or
code or schools. It's about legacy. And
legacy must be practiced before it can be
protected."
Marcus swallowed hard. "Then I better get
to work."
Langston smiled. "Tomorrow. Five a.m."
Marcus groaned. "Five?"
Langston was already halfway to the door.
"Master Chambers would've said four."

Excerpt from ScholarForge Youth
Leadership Session – Newark Chapter
Facilitator: Marcus Baker
Lesson Title: "The Power of the Line –
Naihanchi Chodan"
The training space smelled like sweat, old
mats, and focus.
Ten middle school students stood in
uneven rows, fidgeting with their belts.
Some looked half-asleep. Others looked
like they were waiting for Marcus to tell
them something magical.

He didn't.

Not yet.

Instead, he walked to the center of the floor, barefoot, wearing a ScholarForge hoodie over loose dobok pants. He placed his feet shoulder-width apart, dropped into a deep horse stance, and breathed.

"Naihanchi Chodan," he said, calmly. "I want you to forget how simple it looks. That's where people mess up. They see a straight line and think it's easy."

He scanned the group, then nodded.

"Let me tell you something my mentor—Dr. Langston Graham—told me. This kata isn't about fighting someone in front of you. It's about holding the line when everything is pushing against you from the sides. Distractions. Pressure. Doubt." One boy raised his hand. "But why don't we move forward or turn like in the other forms?"

Marcus smiled.

"Because in life, you won't always get to move. Sometimes you'll be forced to stand your ground. This form teaches you to be unshakable. Your stance, your breath, your focus—it all has to come from inside. If your center isn't strong, you'll collapse from the outside in."

He dropped into the stance again. Each movement came slow, deliberate: inward block, punch, elbow strike, knife-hand. Every step carried the memory of Langston's test on Arch Street. Every exhale was a prayer from Patty Crocker's kitchen.

He finished and stood up straight. "I did
this form for the first time in sneakers on a
cracked sidewalk. I hated it. But I didn't
know that later, when life tested me harder
than any belt exam, this form would
already be in my body. Already
part of my rhythm. I couldn't fall apart—
because I'd already learned how to hold
the line." Silence.
Then the shuffling stopped.
The students dropped into their stances.
Marcus nodded once.
"Now. Let's begin."

Chapter 28 — A New Lost Cause

The rain fell like whispers on the rooftop of Graham Manor, steady and insistent, as though history itself were trying to be heard. Dr. Langston Graham stood in the west library, a place that had grown more sacred with each passing headline. The fire crackled but offered no warmth—only illumination for the article that glowed on his tablet.

"Alabama Governor Signs Bill Banning DEI, Restricting Race-Based Curriculum: Teachers May Be Terminated for 'Divisive Concepts'"

Langston's jaw tightened as he read. He didn't need to scroll. He'd seen this script before—different century, same lines.

He set the tablet down on the mahogany table and walked to the bookshelf near the tall window. His fingers traced the spines until he stopped at one: **"Reconstruction: America's Unfinished Revolution"** by Eric Foner. He opened the worn copy to the pages detailing the 1890s Mississippi textbook purges. He didn't need to read it again, but he needed to *feel* it. Needed to sit with the echo of history.

1890s. Mississippi.

White legislators, fresh off solidifying Jim

Crow with poll taxes and literacy tests,
had turned their sights on the minds of the
young. The legislature passed bills
banning "inflammatory" books from
public schools—anything that spoke
honestly about slavery or that dared call
the Confederacy a rebellion.

Instead, new state-sanctioned textbooks
emerged:
George Washington was presented as
God's anointed.
Robert E. Lee was cast as a martyr of
Southern virtue.
And slavery?
A benign institution that taught
"civilization" to "inferior races."

Langston closed the book and whispered
aloud, "A new Lost Cause."

He returned to his desk and opened his
journal. In bold ink, he began to draft what
would become a ScholarForge
memorandum—but it read like a sermon:

We are not watching history repeat.
We are watching it metastasize.
Alabama's law is not new. It is the
rebirth of textbook tribunals. It is the
hand of 1890 reaching into the minds
of 2025.

Earlier that morning, Monroe had placed a
clipping on his breakfast tray—a quiet act

of care masked as routine. It was a quote from former Tuskegee president Lily McNair:

"This law aims to erase a core history of Americans… There's no reason why we should not understand the history of slavery and racism in America today."

Langston reread those words now. They weren't political—they were ancestral.

He thought of the students at Tuskegee, Alabama State, Miles College—HBCUs carved from segregation's clay and nourished by the belief that truth-telling was a sacred duty. He imagined professors forced to choose between honesty and employment. Imagine teaching Du Bois with a legal noose around your neck.

Imagine banning "The Souls of Black Folk" in Montgomery.

He picked up his phone and called Dr. Malachi Mitchell. The line crackled briefly.

"Langston," Malachi answered, "I was just reading the Alabama bill."

"I know," Langston replied. "I think we're watching the 1890s crawl out of the grave."

Malachi sighed. "They're not trying to ban pain. They're trying to ban the proof of it." Langston said nothing for a moment. Then, "It's not just DEI they're after. It's memory. Literacy. Institutional courage." Malachi's voice sharpened. "We need to respond. ScholarForge has reach."

Langston looked again at the rain-streaked windows. "Then we start with a statement. Not just protest—but pedagogy. If they want to erase, we preserve. If they ban the truth, we amplify it. Loudly."

"And visibly," Malachi added.

Langston smiled grimly. "The louder they legislate, the more we must teach."

That night, he gathered Monroe and Dr. Fountain in the Manor's old salon. On the center table lay copies of old Mississippi textbooks, Tuskegee syllabi, Alabama's new bill, and pages from the 1890s textbook commission records.

Langston handed them both a single typed page.

At the top: **"From Reconstruction to Regression: The New Lost Cause" At the bottom: ScholarForge Emergency Curriculum Protocol No. 12.**

Monroe read it silently, then looked up.

"You want teachers to bypass the law?"
Langston nodded. "We'll call it what it is—supplemental historical context. All online. Open source. Mobile-adaptable. Every banned truth will be reprinted in digital ink."
Fountain smirked. "So, you're opening a bootleg library."

Langston laughed for the first time that day. "Exactly. A bootleg library of the truths they fear most."

And in the bootleg, they would remember.

Not just Alabama. Not just 1890.
But every student taught to question.
Every teacher brave enough to teach anyway.
Every curriculum outlawed because it told the truth.

Langston knew what they were doing in Alabama.

They weren't trying to ban CRT. They were trying to ban CPR—the breath that revives a dying conscience.

But ScholarForge would resist.

And so would the ink.

Chapter 29 — The Mirror Never Cracks

The leather of the study chair cracked faintly beneath Langston Graham as he leaned forward, elbows digging into his knees. The glow from the tablet on the desk reflected faintly in his gold-rimmed glasses. The headline stared back at him, unblinking.

"Two Former Mississippi Deputies Sentenced in Brutal Torture of Black Men: 'They Tried to Take My Manhood,' Survivor Says."

Langston exhaled—long, slow, hollow. He tapped the screen and scrolled.

Matthew Clark Johnson and Emmett Tyrone Phillips. Their names now etched into the catalog of American terror. Two Black men. Brutalized, humiliated, nearly executed by lawmen who carried the state's seal on their badges and hatred in their hearts.

The article read like a confession—except the monsters didn't repent. They grinned. They mocked. They texted each other in the group chat they named *"The Thug Squad."*

Langston rose and crossed the room, boots silent on the old Persian rug. He stood by the library's west-facing window. Beyond the glass, the manicured gardens lay quiet beneath dusk. But his mind wasn't in the present. Not fully. Not now.

1955. Money, Mississippi.

The memory wasn't personal, but it was encoded. Cultural DNA. Ancestral recall.

Emmett Till.
Fourteen. Black. Accused of whistling at a white woman.
Dragged from bed, tortured, shot, and dumped like a warning.
And the woman—safe in her lie. The killers—safe in their whiteness. The jury—sworn to silence and kinship, not justice.

Langston pressed his fingers to the cold glass. Some people called that *the past*— as if it had been laid to rest.

But the past wasn't resting.

It was kneeling on Johnsons' chest, pouring syrup over his face while deputies laughed.

It was in the gun shoved in Johnsons' mouth, the trigger pulled in mock execution, the shot ripping through flesh not fiction.

It was in the shower stall, where deputies forced the men to strip and wash themselves like slaves scrubbing away shame while overseers watched.

It was in the cover-up, the planted drugs, the forged police reports, the "good ol' boy" silence. All rehearsed. All perfected over centuries.

The only difference was the timestamp.

Langston returned to his desk and opened a drawer. Inside: a worn photograph. His grandmother, Patty Crocker, clutching a battered copy of *Jet* magazine. Emmett's mutilated face stared out from the cover, black and white but bleeding into every decade that followed.

She'd told him once:

"They don't just kill the body, Lang. They kill the dignity first. That way, the grave feels justified."

He hadn't understood then. He did now.

He flipped open his leather-bound journal, the one Dr. Fountain had commissioned with handmade Moroccan paper and gilt-edged corners. It had become more than a journal—a vault of reckoning.

"They tried to take my manhood."

Langston wrote the words slowly, deliberately. They belonged to Johnson, but they echoed from centuries of violated Black bodies—auction blocks, convict leasing, prison buses, traffic stops.

He continued:
1955: Emmett Till.
2023: Matthew Johnson.
Still punished for proximity to whiteness.
Still presumed guilty.
Still buried—if not in graves, then in
trauma.

He turned to a fresh page and began
outlining his next lecture. Not for students
this time, but for the ScholarForge
convening. He had already been asked to
deliver a keynote titled *"Memory as
Resistance."* This—this would be the
centerpiece.

The Mirror Never Cracks: From Till to Johnson

"We claim progress. We count laws, not
scars. But the mirror of this country never
cracks. It reflects the same face—
different badge, newer weapon, same lie.
They said Emmett was 'out of line.' They
said Johnson 'didn't belong.' What they
mean is:
Black men still require permission.
To live.
To exist.
To survive proximity to whiteness. But
we don't need permission. We need
protection." Langston's hand trembled
slightly as he set the pen down. He
stared at the ink. Still wet. Still honest.

He imagined Johnson, no longer able to sing—his voice stolen by a trigger. Phillips, too terrified to speak in court. Their attorney had read their words. But trauma, Langston knew, wasn't always translatable. Some wounds lived in silence.

He reached for the remote and turned on the stereo. Mingus filled the study. *II B.S.*—raw, unfiltered jazz, defiant and irreverent. The soundtrack of unburied truth.

Monroe's footsteps padded down the corridor. She'd bring tea soon. She always knew when his spirit was weighted. She never intruded, only anchored.

But tonight, Langston would not speak.

He would remember.

And in that remembering, resist.

Chapter 30: The Ashes and the Atlas

Wounds do not vanish. They speak—through silence, through ritual, through fire.

The Atlas Club stood as a quiet citadel nestled in the Virginia suburbs just outside D.C.—a fortress of polished restraint and legacy. Its founder, Kevin Greene—a brilliant entrepreneur and quiet strategist—stood on the shoulders of surgeons, diplomats, and civil rights lawyers. Black men of distinction who knew the cost of entry into the halls of power and still chose to carve their own. Greene took their blueprints and built what they only dreamed of: an institution that taught truth without apology and forged legacy without permission. Langston Graham often said the Atlas was the only place in America where bourbon flowed as freely as honesty among Black intellectuals. Through entrepreneur Kevin Greene, the club had become an unofficial embassy of the mind—where ideas were currency, and silence was a violation of trust. Langston, ever the gentleman scholar, discreetly ensured the humidor remained stocked with the finest Cuban cigars, acquired through a network of friends who understood that liberation sometimes came wrapped in tobacco leaves and whispered in wood-paneled rooms. Greene's vision for the Atlas honored the legacy. The Atlas wasn't just a club. It was a forge.

Inside the private study, jazz murmured softly from a live trio tucked in the corner. A slow, contemplative rendition of Coltrane's *Naima* played under the hum of firelight and the rustle of pages from half read books. The air was rich with sandalwood, dark liquor, and the smoke of serious cigars.

Obadiah sat with a straight spine in a worn leather chair, his silhouette flickering with the fire. In one hand, a cigar smoldered with resolve. In the other, a heavy bottomed glass of bourbon remained untouched.

"You know," he began, voice deliberate and low, "when they bombed that church in Birmingham, they didn't just kill four little girls. They shattered the illusion that Sunday morning was sacred. Even our worship became a battlefield."

Langston nodded slowly. He had removed his gold signet ring and was rolling it between his fingers—a small ritual he returned to when the past refused to stay quiet.

"Addie Mae. Denise. Carole. Cynthia," he recited. "Little girls who never lived long

enough to see their dreams betray them.
Buried in rubble, under stained glass,
beneath the notes of gospel hymns."
He paused. "And still, that congregation
showed up the next Sunday. Still wearing
grief like pressed linen." Obadiah leaned
forward slightly. "And fifty-two years
later, they walked right back into the fire.
Charleston. Mother Emanuel. He sat with
them, Langston. For forty-five minutes.
Prayed with them. Laughed with them.
Studied scripture with them. Then stood
up during the benediction—and turned the
room into a graveyard."

Langston set his glass down on a law book
and spoke softly. "He didn't choose just
any church. He chose *that* church.
Founded in resistance. Burned to the
ground for hosting slave uprisings. Rebuilt
by faith and brick. The oldest Black
church in the South."

"And he walked in like he belonged
there," Obadiah added. "That's the part I
can't shake. They welcomed him. Offered
him a seat. A prayer. A place. And he
repaid it with a massacre."

Langston nodded. "He weaponized our
hospitality. Our grace."

Obadiah stood and walked toward the
large window, brushing back the velvet
curtain. The city lights of D.C. were faint
in the distance, a constellation of power
and pretense.

"They keep saying these are isolated incidents," he said, his voice sharper now. "Lone wolves, bad apples, mental illness. As if 1963 didn't whisper 2015 in plain English. As if Black churches haven't always been seen as insurrectionary just for existing."

Langston joined him, standing tall. "And as if the danger ended at the door. Today they don't have to bomb churches—they just defund them. Strip protections. Ban Black history from classrooms. Starve equity programs. It's all quieter now. But not softer."

Obadiah looked at him, eyes smoldering. "It's legislative violence in a Brooks Brothers suit."

Langston gave a dry laugh. "You would know."

Obadiah smirked. "Touché."

They returned to their chairs, but neither sat. Obadiah tapped ash from the end of his cigar and spoke again.

"You ever think forgiveness is the only virtue they'll tolerate from us? Not truth. Not defiance. Not demands. Just grief wrapped in gospel lyrics and offered with bowed heads."

Langston's gaze didn't waver. "I think forgiveness, when freely given, is powerful. But when expected—or demanded—it becomes performance. One that lets the real perpetrators offstage before the curtain drops."

Obadiah nodded. "Douglas Rufner didn't ask for mercy. He said he had to do it. That he wanted to start a race war. And what did America do? Took down a flag. Gave some hugs. Then moved on."

Langston's voice dropped. "Not all of us moved on. Some of us carried the funeral programs in our briefcases. We teach their names like scripture."

He lifted his hand and placed the signet ring back on his finger. The light caught its crest.

"You know," he continued, "sometimes I worry our people have been trained to grieve so well that we've forgotten how to demand."

Obadiah didn't respond immediately. He exhaled a long breath of smoke and let it drift toward the rafters. "We're not broken," he said at last. "But we are conditioned. Conditioned to mourn, to rebuild, to move on—but not always to confront."

He tapped his temple.

"That's why memory matters. That's why history matters. That's why every banned book, every silenced professor, every redistricted vote—they all point to the same agenda: control the narrative, erase the blood."

Langston walked over to the bookshelf and pulled out an old worn copy of *The Fire Next Time*. He opened it reverently. "They're not afraid of riots," he said. "They're afraid of memory. Because memory ties it all together. From Emmett Till to Trayvon. From Birmingham to Charleston. From colored-only fountains to voter suppression apps."

The jazz trio paused, replaced by the low hiss of the fireplace.

Langston turned toward Obadiah. "Do you believe we're making progress?"

Obadiah's eyes narrowed—not in anger, but in calculation. "Progress bends. It's slow. It stalls. But memory? Memory's sharper than progress. More honest. It doesn't need permission to tell the truth." He raised his glass.

"To the ones who didn't survive… and the ones who refuse to forget."

Langston raised his in reply. "Ashes don't scatter in silence. Not anymore."

They drank slowly, not in celebration, but in consecration. The silence that followed wasn't hollow. It was sacred.

Chapter 31: The Weight of Water

The room was dim, but not due to lack of light. The blinds were drawn halfway, casting long shadows over the room's wood-paneled walls. The air held the quiet stillness of a courtroom, though this was no courthouse—it was Langston Graham's seminar on Policy, Power, and the People.

The students were unusually subdued. A headline had broken that morning: *Another child dead in Flint. 2023.* The mother, a Black woman named Regina Washington, had lost both of her sons to complications tied to lead exposure. They were ten and twelve when the poisoning began.

Langston stood at the head of the seminar table, his left hand resting on a thick folder labeled "Flint – Case Studies," and his right-hand scribbling something in the margins of *The Southern Floods: 1927 and the Making of the New Jim Crow.*

He looked up. "We're going to talk today about water. Not as a resource—but as a weapon."

A few students stirred in their seats.

He turned on the projector. Two side-by side headlines appeared:

*• Detroit Free Press, 2023: Flint
Mother Buries Second Child From
Lead Exposure •
The Crisis Magazine,
1927:
Negroes Left to Die in Delta Flood*

Langston's voice was calm, but the undercurrent in it was firm steel. "Most of you have read about the Flint Water Crisis. But you may not have studied the 1927 Mississippi Flood. And yet, the same fingerprints are on both."

He pointed to the older headline.

"In 1927, the Mississippi River broke through levees and drowned hundreds of thousands of acres. Hundreds of Black laborers were ordered—at gunpoint—to remain on the levees, stacking sandbags to protect white-owned towns. When the waters rose, the Black quarters were sacrificed. Refugees were corralled into camps. Some were never seen again." The students stared, stunned.

Langston clicked the remote again. Now, an image of Flint residents holding bottled water outside a courthouse.

"In Flint, 2014, an emergency manager—appointed, not elected—authorized switching Flint's water source to the Flint River. No corrosion control. No safeguards. The state of Michigan claimed it was safe. But children began getting rashes. Hair fell out. Pipes turned orange. Lead levels soared. And what did the state say?"

He paused. "They said, 'It's fine.' Just like they did in 1927."

A student named Devon raised his hand slowly. "Professor Graham… are you saying Flint was intentional?"

Langston nodded gravely. "Intentional doesn't always mean someone twisted a villainous mustache in a boardroom. Intentional means the warnings were there—and they were ignored. It means that when the choice came down to cost or community, they chose cost. And it means that because those people were poor and Black, they assumed no one would make noise. That's intentional neglect."

Another student, Marisol, whispered, "And they were right… no one really paid."

Langston folded his hands. "One low-level official. That's it. One. Meanwhile, thousands of children were poisoned, and some families will never be whole again."

He stepped closer to the table, resting his palms flat against its oak surface. "Let me ask you this—what do Flint and the 1927 Flood have in common?"

Silence.
Then, Marcus—sitting in the back—
spoke. "They both made Black suffering
seem... logistical. Acceptable loss."

Langston nodded, lips tight. "Yes. Exactly.
Both events showed us that in the eyes of
the powerful, the lives of the poor—
especially poor Black lives—were
expendable in pursuit of control, image, or
profit."

He clicked once more. The final slide
showed two maps:

- One of the levee breach zones in
  the Delta.
- One of the neighborhoods in Flint
  with the highest recorded lead
  levels.

Over 90% of the affected zones in both
maps were majority Black.

Langston's voice softened. "This isn't just
about history. This is about memory.
Policy memory. Institutional memory.
Flint happened because the people in
charge had forgotten—or never learned—
that Black communities remember. We
remember the floods. We remember the
pipelines. We remember the poison."

He closed the laptop and stepped away.

"History doesn't repeat itself. It rhymes—
because the same machinery is still

running. But what if we stopped being cogs? What if we became architects?" Marcus leaned forward. "You mean… ScholarForge?"

Langston smiled, faintly. "Yes. ScholarForge was never just about data encryption or underground education. It was about control of narrative. Of protecting memory—not just preserving it."

He reached into his leather satchel and retrieved a worn booklet—*The Negro Silent Protest Parade Program, 1917.* "Because when the waters rise—and they always do—it's the ones who've learned to build the levees of truth that hold the line."

As the students filed out, silent and charged, Langston remained behind, watching the final headline flicker once more:

We the Poisoned — and still, no justice.

"The Smell of Iron and Mud"

Setting: Trenton, New Jersey – Summer of
1983
Characters: Young Langston (age 13),
Grandma Patty

The box fan in the window rattled like a
tired train. It was one of those heavy
Trenton summers—thick air, still rooms,
and water you didn't trust straight from the
tap.

Young Langston sat cross-legged on the
floor, flipping through a library copy of
Popular Mechanics, the corners bent
and faded. In the kitchen, Grandma
Patty stirred a pot of greens, the old
radio humming a gospel station between
bouts of static.

Langston stood and wandered over to the
kitchen sink. He twisted the faucet and let
the water run. A sharp, metallic scent
drifted upward.

"Smell that?" he asked.

Patty didn't even look up. "Iron. Pipes are
old," she said, almost like a reflex. Then,
after a pause: "Don't drink from that one
unless you boil it first."

Langston frowned. "Why?" She turned off the burner and walked over, her apron dusted with flour. "Because nobody ever cared if these buildings had clean water. Same way they didn't care back when I was little."

She leaned against the counter. "We had cousins in the Delta when the river broke in '27. Whole Black towns gone overnight. Water took everything— houses, mules, children. And when the levees gave way, guess who got rescued last?"
Langston stared at the stream still trickling from the faucet. "They let that happen?"

"They *made* it happen, baby. They sent the flood toward us to save the white towns. Called it strategy."

She looked hard at him now, her voice low and firm. "That's why we don't just trust what comes out the tap. Not then. Not now."

Langston turned off the water. "How come people don't fix it?"

She smiled—but it didn't reach her eyes. *"Because the pipes might be broken, but so's the system. And the system's got plumbers who only come when it's their own house leaking."*

Langston didn't say anything. But he remembered that smell—metal and mold

and memory. It would come back to him
years later, in the basement of
ScholarForge, when he held a corroded
pipe from Newark in one hand and a flash
drive of testimonies in the other.

Chapter 32: Two Gifts, One Problem

Langston Graham sat on the veranda, staring at two photographs laid side by side on his desk.

One was sleek and modern—a luxury jet, outfitted with cream leather, gold fixtures, and a hushed interior built for kings. The image had appeared just days ago in a business journal, celebrating former President David Thomas' "new ride"—a gift from a coalition of private donors who admired his "service to the nation." There were no hearings. No ethics investigation. No consequences.

The other photo was older. Grainy. A black-and-white still of Imam Khalid Rahman, standing before a modest podium, flanked by members of his community. Behind him, a crowd of supporters—Black, Brown, Muslim, Christian, young and old. Beneath the photo, the headline:

"U.S. Blocks $1 Billion Gift to American Muslim Leader from Libya." Langston leaned back in his chair and exhaled through his nose. There was a difference between contradiction and hypocrisy. Contradiction was a human mistake. Hypocrisy required planning. He picked up the folder Monroe had left earlier that

morning. Inside were several clippings—
editorials, analysis, a timeline.

But Langston needed only one paragraph.
He read aloud, voice low but steady:
"The gift, a $1 billion pledge from Libyan
President Khouri, intended for schools,
housing, and Black-owned enterprises
across major U.S. cities, was frozen under
U.S. sanctions—citing national security
and fears of foreign influence." He set the
paper down and turned toward Marcus
Baker, who stood just inside the doorway.
"You ever heard of Imam Rahman's
billion-dollar gift?"

Marcus furrowed his brow. "No, sir."

Langston nodded. "Most people haven't.
They scrubbed it before it could take
root."

He tapped the grainy photo. "1996. Imam
Rahman had just finished a historic
goodwill tour—meeting with heads of
state in Ghana, Egypt, South Africa, and
Libya. In Tripoli, President Khouri
pledged $1 billion—not to fund
extremism, but to build schools in
Detroit, clinics in Baltimore, credit unions
in

Oakland. A Marshall Plan for Black
America."

Marcus looked stunned. "A billion
dollars?"

Langston nodded slowly. "Do you know
what that kind of capital injection could've
meant for us? A generation of college
students could've attended debt-free.
Entrepreneurs could've launched their

businesses without SBA red tape. Entire blocks of families could've owned homes—before gentrification priced them out."

He leaned forward, his voice tightening. "We talk about student loan defaults like it's a moral failing. But it's policy. It's design. Had that money reached our communities, you wouldn't see tens of thousands of Black and Brown graduates crushed by debt. You'd see them building wealth. Circulating dollars. Contributing more to the economy than the government ever feared."

Marcus asked softly, "So why stop it?"

Langston's eyes locked on his. "Because to some people, Black prosperity is more dangerous than Black poverty. Poverty they can manage—control, exploit. But economic sovereignty? They see that as a threat to the existing order." He rose and pointed toward the image of Steele's jet. "And meanwhile, President Steele walks away with a luxury aircraft—gifted by oil magnates, foreign investors, and media conglomerates. No headlines screaming foreign interference. No Treasury agents freezing accounts. It's just... 'gratitude.'"

Langston stepped toward the window, rain tapping softly against the glass. "They don't fear money, Marcus. They fear what happens when we don't need theirs."

Silence settled between them. Langston turned back and handed Marcus the folder.

"This is what you need to understand. ScholarForge isn't just a school—it's a firewall against that kind of sabotage. They don't just want to keep us undereducated. They want to keep us undercapitalized. That's how control is maintained."

Marcus took the folder in both hands, more carefully than before. Langston lowered his voice. "They will tolerate our ambition—so long as it's channeled through them. But the moment we fund ourselves, own our schools, pay our debts, build our cities... they panic. Because we prove we never needed permission. Just opportunity." As Marcus turned to leave, Langston whispered to the room behind him:

"One jet was a threat.

The other was a trophy.

And both tell the truth about the country we live in."

Chapter 33: A Promise in the Quiet

Evening settled gently over the quiet suburb outside Washington, D.C., where the sound of distant traffic was muffled by oaks and manicured hedges. The Graham home stood with the quiet dignity of a place lived in by thinkers—a brick Georgian with ivy trailing one side and tall windows that caught the last blush of sunset.

On the back terrace, Sabrina Graham sat curled into a wicker chaise, wrapped in a cream shawl that had belonged to her mother. The wine in her glass had gone warm. The novel in her lap hadn't moved past page twelve. Her gaze was fixed on the line where the backyard met the tree line—a perfect horizon, undisturbed and unchanging. Unlike her days.

Inside the house, muted voices hummed behind glass. Langston's tone rose and fell like a professor giving a lecture he knew too well. Monroe's British cadence responded with crisp efficiency. Sabrina didn't need to hear the details. She already knew: Morocco. Fez. Hand-bound journals. Another mission. Another trip.

Another postponement.
She exhaled quietly and picked up the wine, but didn't drink it. Instead, she let

her fingers trace the rim of the glass as her thoughts wandered—to a different season in their life. Before the world pressed in. Before Monroe became a fixture. Before Langston's study was a war room. When it was just them, talking about philosophy and recipes and dreams they hadn't yet given away to the public good.

He came out eventually, his frame filling the doorway as the last of the sun kissed his face. He wore his usual: soft-pressed trousers, button-down shirt, a navy linen blazer he claimed helped him "think more clearly." His tie was already loose. But he didn't look at ease. Not really.

"You heard," he said, voice softer than the wind.

"I did," she replied, not looking away from the horizon. "Every word."

Langston stepped onto the terrace and sat beside her without invitation. He didn't offer a defense—he knew better.

"I won't be long," he said. "A few days, that's all. Monroe found a binder in Fez— some old artisan who still uses camel hide and hand-dyed thread. It's a disappearing craft. Same binding as the Wellspring book we archived last year."

Sabrina gave the smallest nod. "Sounds important."

"It is," he said. "But it's not more important than—"
"Don't finish that sentence, Langston," she interrupted, calm but sharp. "Because you always say that. Right before you leave again."

He looked at her now, really looked. The way he used to when she walked into his classroom back when he was just "Professor Graham" and she was completing her second graduate degree. She wasn't just a partner then—she was a spark, an equal, a mirror.

"You're right," he said. "I've been… everywhere but here."

She finally turned to face him, her expression unreadable. "I know what you're building, Langston. I do. ScholarForge is needed. These journals, these files, these secret gatherings— they're saving lives. I see it. But sometimes I wonder if you've forgotten that *we* had plans too. You and me. A life. A rhythm."

He swallowed hard. "I haven't forgotten."

"You've deferred it," she said. "You give the world your mind, your presence, your defiance. You give Monroe your time and your trust. And I get the leftovers. Late night returns. Missed dinners. A wave from the study."
Langston stood and paced slowly, hands in his pockets. The air had cooled now, and a

few cicadas had begun their nightly chorus.

"You know I trust you," she said, rising to stand beside him. "It's not about Monroe. She's brilliant. Loyal. She's saved your life more than once. But she's not your wife."

He turned to her. "And she never will be."

There was silence.

Then he took her hand, slowly, reverently, as if re-learning her touch. "When I get back, you name the night. The hour. The place. I'll wear what you choose. Say yes to anything. No distractions. Just us."

"No journal in your pocket?"

"Not even a pen."

"No coded language? No Monroe decoding facial expressions from across the room?"

Langston smiled. "Just me. And you."

"You promise?"

He raised her hand to his lips and kissed her wrist—gently, deliberately, like a benediction. "On the family crest."
Sabrina rolled her eyes but smiled. "You and that crest. Langston, you'd swear on your shoelaces if they had a Latin motto."

"*Per veritatem ascendimus,*" he said solemnly. "By truth, we rise." She laughed despite herself and leaned into him, her head resting against his shoulder. "Just come back to me. Not just physically. Come back whole. I miss that man."

Langston closed his eyes and breathed her in—the familiar scent of lavender and something warmer, steadier. "I'm still him. I've just… been chasing shadows." "Then stop. Even for one night. Stop."

The lights from the neighbor's porch blinked off. The street fell quiet. Somewhere in the house, Langston's phone buzzed again, but neither of them moved. For now, for this breath of a moment, time stood still.

And when he left for Fez the next morning, she didn't cry. She didn't argue. She kissed him deeply at the airport curb, looked him in the eye, and said, "Make it count. Then come home." And he promised—again.

But this time, he meant to keep it.

Chapter 34: The Line Goes Public

The auditorium buzzed.
The ScholarForge National Symposium had never felt like this before—press passes, livestream cameras, dignitaries seated alongside high school seniors and local barbers. The theme that year was "Sovereignty Through Learning." But nobody expected the most powerful message to come from the youngest name on the schedule.

Marcus Baker adjusted the mic, cleared his throat, and looked out at the crowd. Langston watched quietly from the back of the room, arms crossed, his expression unreadable. Monroe stood beside him, pearl earrings subtle, tailored blazer sharp. She gave Marcus a barely perceptible nod—the kind that meant: Make it count. But before the speech, there had been the suit.

Three days earlier, Langston and Monroe had taken Marcus to Brooks Brothers. He'd never stepped foot in a store like that. The air itself smelled like polished wood and quiet money. His fingers hesitated over the lapels. Langston held up a navy jacket. "Super 120s wool. Classic. Not loud, not soft. Just like you." Monroe adjusted the hem, checking the mirror. "We'll have the trousers cuffed. Slim taper. You'll look like an institution."

Marcus blinked at the reflection. "This is… a lot."

Langston gave him a half smile. "No. This is overdue."

As Marcus stood now, centered beneath the stage lights in ScholarForge gold and navy, Langston's mind drifted—just for a second—to his grandmother, Patty Crocker. Her voice echoed like a hymn whispered through time:

"Put that suit on with your spine straight, baby. That fabric's expensive, but your legacy's priceless."

He didn't smile. He didn't need to. The memory sat with him, warm and steady. Marcus didn't use a teleprompter. He barely glanced at the podium. The words were alive inside him now—rooted deep, like Naihanchi Chodan stances etched into muscle memory. "Good afternoon. My name is Marcus Baker. I'm a ScholarForge fellow. I'm also a former foster kid, a survivor of public-school neglect, and a first-generation college student drowning in debt for a degree that opened the door but didn't guarantee a seat. And today, I want to talk about two opportunities."

The audience fell silent.

"In 1996, Imam Khalid Rahman was offered a $1 billion gift from Libyan President Khouri. A fund to build schools, banks, and businesses in Black and Brown communities across America. What did the U.S. government do? They blocked it. Froze the funds. Labeled it foreign interference. Said empowerment was dangerous if it came from the wrong direction.

But years later, former President David Thomas received a custom private jet from billionaires. No hearings. No sanctions. No scrutiny.

So, I ask you: Why is one opportunity a threat, and the other a trophy? What kind of country fears Black independence more than it fears corruption?

What kind of nation would rather watch us default on loans than allow us to fund our own futures?"

Gasps rippled through the audience. Cameras zoomed in.

Langston leaned forward ever so slightly. "If that $1 billion had been allowed to land, we might not be talking about student loan forgiveness—we'd be talking about student loan freedom. We'd be debating how many Black-owned banks had doubled, not how many corner stores had closed.

We'd be calculating mortgages, not minimum payments.

But there are those—some in this room, some watching online—who find that vision dangerous. They don't fear charity. They fear sovereignty. That's why ScholarForge exists. We are not building an educational program.

We are building an exit strategy." By now, the standing ovation had already begun—first in the front rows, then up the aisles. Langston remained still. But something behind his eyes flickered.

Recognition. Continuity. The applause was thunderous. But the backlash was faster.

By that evening, conservative think tanks were denouncing the speech as "radical anti-American rhetoric." News anchors used words like "ungrateful" and "conspiratorial." Donor emails to ScholarForge slowed. Anonymous threats ticked upward.

But so did scholarship applications.

The video—titled "Two Opportunities, One Nation"—hit 4.2 million views in 36 hours. High school seniors from Detroit, Puerto Rico, the Bronx, and rural Alabama stitched their own responses to it. Some reposted it with tears. Others with fire.

Inside the walls of Graham Manor, Langston poured two glasses of water. Handed one to Marcus.

"You knew what that would cause," he said flatly.

Marcus nodded. "I did."

Langston raised his glass. "Then welcome to the fire."

They drank in silence.

Outside, the storm had just begun.

Chapter 35: Bones Beneath the Laurels

It was the kind of story that barely made the national news.

Buried beneath a headline about the Dow Jones and a feature on a missing influencer was a quiet, almost clinical press release: "Peer-reviewed archaeological findings confirm the discovery of 28 possible graves belonging to enslaved individuals at Andrew Jackson's Hermitage estate." Langston sat at the edge of the long oak conference table at Graham Manor, a leather-bound journal open, a pen resting in the crease. The rain tapped the windows like hesitant truth.

He didn't flinch at the number. Twenty-eight. Not shocking. Not even surprising. He had grown numb to America's belated discoveries—its ability to exhume horror centuries after the headlines had moved on. What struck him wasn't the number. It was the distance. A thousand feet northwest of the Hermitage mansion. That's how far they had to be buried. Not beside the family that had owned their bodies. Not near the marble tombs with etchings and epitaphs. A thousand feet—a literal separation of memory. A topography of erasure. "Bones beneath the laurels," he murmured, writing the phrase in his journal.

The report detailed how invasive foliage had to be cleared, how irregular patches of limestone marked sunken ground, how ground-penetrating radar helped validate the presence of burial sites without disturbing them. Langston read every word, not as a historian, but as a descendant of ghosts.

"This is how America handles truth," he said aloud. "With fencing. With gravel paths and signage."

Across the table, Monroe was silent. She had brought him the article that morning, printed neatly, folded once, laid beside his coffee. She knew his ritual: read, absorb, brood, speak. She waited for the spark. It always came.

"It's not just archaeology," Langston continued. "It's a metaphor. The country keeps rediscovering its sins like they're fossils. But these were people. Not bones. Not data points. People who bent under the lash and prayed for breath, now reappearing just outside the main house. Still denied the front porch." He flipped to a new page and began sketching the layout of the Hermitage property as described in the report—the tree line, the slight rise above Sinking Creek, the undisturbed land that had kept their resting place intact. It reminded him of what his grandmother used to say: "The land remembers what men forget." The more he thought, the more he saw the pattern. The discovery in 2024 hadn't come from government initiative or national reckoning—it came from private benefactors, a few tenacious historians, and archaeologists who read maps and aerial photos like sacred texts. Truth, as always, had to be hunted down. Verified.

Peer-reviewed. Made palatable.

Even then, it was fenced off.

Langston looked up.

"Do you know what this really is?" he asked Monroe.

She gave a gentle shake of her head. "It's an unpaid debt," he said. "A ledger entry left open. We're standing in the present with the past knocking under our feet."

He thought about how his own students treated history as something that happened and ended. But here—here was proof that the past had a pulse. That it refused to be buried properly because it never had been.

Langston stood and moved toward the tall window that overlooked the back garden. The fog curled around the hedges like mourning clothes. He imagined standing at that newly discovered site in Tennessee—not as a tourist, but as a witness.

Chapter 36: What If the Nation Had Said Yes

Langston stood at the edge of the granite memorial fountain inside the ScholarForge campus, hands behind his back, eyes tracing the ripple patterns that danced beneath the bronze plaque: "In honor of the unseen architects — those who built futures in the dark, hoping the sun would one day rise."

Marcus leaned against the opposite side of the fountain, arms folded. "You ever wonder what it would've looked like?"

Langston raised an eyebrow. "The world," Marcus clarified. "If we'd accepted the billion."

Langston didn't answer right away. He pulled a folded page from his jacket — an old article, laminated and creased with time.

1996: Libyan President Khouri Offers $1B to Fund Black Empowerment. U.S. Freezes Funds, Cites National Security.

Langston handed it over without a word. Marcus read the headline, then looked up slowly. "They called it interference."

Langston's voice was low and deliberate. "Of course they did. Because if we ever got a real head start — not just survival money, but transformation money — the system couldn't absorb the fallout." He

walked slowly toward a nearby bench and sat. "Imagine the alternative," he said, voice firm now. "One billion dollars directed into historically neglected communities. Hundreds of tuition-free academies. Microloans for Black-owned startups. Mortgage subsidies for first-generation homeowners. Credit unions not controlled by Wall Street. We could've cut the Black student loan default rate in half within ten years." Marcus nodded, imagining it. Langston continued. "By now? The second generation would be inheriting equity, not debt. Homelessness would've plummeted. College would feel like preparation — not punishment." He paused. "But that terrified them." Marcus lowered his head. "You think that's why they really blocked it?" Langston's eyes didn't blink. "Power fears independence. And independence funded from outside the empire? That's revolution."
He pointed up at the ScholarForge dome, shimmering against the dusk. "This? What we built here? It's the shadow of what could've been. We're standing in the echo of a dream someone else killed before it took its first breath."
There was silence, heavy but electric.
Then Marcus asked the question that had lingered in the hearts of millions: "If we'd taken that gift, would kids still be drowning in student debt today?"
Langston's jaw tightened. "Not like this. Not with interest compounding like shackles. Not with parents afraid to cosign because they already lost a home in '08.

Not with college graduates serving food instead of building futures." "And homelessness?" Langston nodded grimly. "A billion invested in housing infrastructure, wraparound services, job creation? We'd have seen real drops. Not PR campaigns. Not empty shelters. Real change." Marcus exhaled, slow and heavy. "So, what do we do now?" Langston stood. His voice cut like scripture:
"We educate. We organize. We document. And we never let them write us out of our own liberation again."
He folded the article and placed it in the inside pocket of his blazer, right next to his heart.
"The next offer may not come from Libya. But when it does — we'll be ready to say yes."

Chapter 37: The Fabric of Strategy

The lights in the Capitol hearing room burned with surgical precision—clinical, cold, and intentional. Rows of dark suits lined the gallery like sentinels. Cameras hummed. Pens scratched. Phones recorded.

Langston Graham didn't fidget. He never did. He sat still as stone, his notes arranged in geometric calm, his gold rimmed glasses reflecting the buzz of government theater.

At the head of the panel sat Charles Norrington, sleeves rolled with curated informality, voice slick with a salesman's luster. To the untrained eye, Norrington appeared relaxed. But Monroe, seated just behind Langston with a legal pad in her lap and no pen in hand, read the micro tension in his jawline. He was hunting, not hosting.

"Let's be clear, Dr. Graham," Norrington began, tapping his folder with two fingers. "No one's talking about mass deportation. We're proposing a pilot program—outsourcing long-term incarceration to a facility in El Salvador. Cost-saving. Controlled. Fully compliant with international standards."

Langston didn't blink. "You're proposing to remove American citizens—many convicted of non-violent offenses—from their constitutional rights and ship them out of the country like surplus cargo."

A murmur passed through the gallery. Norrington leaned back in his chair, casually flipping a page in his packet.

"The reality, Doctor, is that we're simply thinking outside the box. Some boxes, I admit, are made of steel and concrete, but they're still costly. Taxpayers are tired. Innovation is overdue."

Langston raised an eyebrow. "Innovation at the expense of liberty is not innovation. It's treason in a new suit."

The room tightened.

Norrington smirked, the cue for a pivot. "Tell me something, Dr. Graham—do you ever wonder how many of the people you claim to fight for can afford that suit you wear? Brooks Brothers, isn't it? It's fascinating—how rebellion always seems to come dressed in the very fabric of the establishment."

A few chuckles. One aide scribbled it down. The soundbite had landed. Langston adjusted his cuffs with the reverence of ritual, then stood. The lighting caught the subtle luster of his camel-hair blazer, the perfectly knotted silk tie—ScholarForge gold. He stepped forward.

"I wear Brooks Brothers for the same reason I quote Frederick Douglass in rooms lined with oil paintings of slaveowners.

To remind them—

Their traditions don't intimidate me.

They inform my strategy."

The air left the room like breath withheld.

Monroe allowed herself the faintest smile. Just enough to say: Now you've done it. Langston moved to the center microphone, unshaken. He could feel the eyes—supporters, skeptics, cameras that would turn this moment into a headline before sundown.

"This isn't about policy," he said. "It's about precedent. Today you outsource prisoners. Tomorrow, you outsource justice. What happens when a man in Georgia is sentenced by a judge in Texas to serve time in El Salvador? What happens when that man never returns—not because he escaped, but because the system made it more profitable to forget him?"

Norrington leaned forward. "You're making it sound like we're building a gulag."

Langston's voice cooled, sharp as glass. "I'm saying that if the Constitution no longer protects people you don't like, it no longer protects anyone at all." He let that hang.

"You want to save money?" he continued. "Then end the prison-industrial complex. Decriminalize poverty. Forgive debts you created through predatory lending and discriminatory policing. But don't disguise human trafficking as fiscal policy."

Norrington interrupted, voice clipped. "We are not trafficking—"

"You're exporting bodies for profit," Langston said. "You just found a way to do it in a three-piece suit." Silence.

The phrase landed like a closing argument—and a verdict. Langston gathered his notes. He didn't rush. He looked to Monroe, who gave the barest nod—go.

And as he reached the door, without turning back, he spoke just loud enough: "If they ever build that prison in El Salvador—

Make sure they leave room for the Constitution.

Because once you do this, that's what you'll have to bury there." Then he left.

The door clicked shut. And for several seconds, no one spoke.

Later That Day — Graham Manor The news had already exploded. #ThreePieceGulag trended by noon. #GrahamvNorrington by 1:00 p.m. By 3:30, a White House spokesperson had issued a carefully worded statement distancing the administration from "unauthorized penal policy speculation." Langston stood in his study, jacket draped over the wingback chair, shirtsleeves rolled just once. Monroe watched from the doorway, arms crossed.

"They're calling it a security innovation," she said. "CNN just gave the segment a neutral rating."

Langston exhaled slowly. "The middle always calls genocide a misunderstanding—until it's too late." She walked to the desk and set down a printed photo. It showed a group of young men, mostly Black and Latino, chained at the ankles, boarding a transport bus. The photo was from 2019.

"They're still trying to say this is about saving money," she said. Langston looked at the image. He didn't flinch. "No," he replied. "It's about saving a system that needs people in cages to survive."

A storm brewed outside. And inside, the war was only beginning.

Chapter 38: Public Outcry

The studio lights blazed, cool against the red-white-blue set of American Accountability Tonight. At the desk sat Charles Norrington — conservative firebrand, Yale-educated moralist, and unapologetic cultural commentator — his fingers steepled in front of him as the camera panned in.

"This... this is what hypocrisy looks like," he began, his voice smooth as lacquer but pulsing with contempt. "Dr. Langston Elkanah Graham. A so-called public intellectual. A man who built an education platform praised in the New York Times, who lectures on moral accountability, who walks through elite institutions in soft shouldered Brooks Brothers suits and handmade English shoes — and yet, can't be bothered to pay back a dime of his federal student loans." The chyron at the bottom of the screen read:

"ELITE ENTITLEMENT: LANGSTON GRAHAM REFUSES TO PAY HIS DEBT"

Norrington leaned forward, adjusting his cufflinks — gold, understated, smug. "Let me break this down," he said. "The average American teacher makes about $56,000 a year. They pay taxes. They honor their commitments. They raise children. And when those student loan bills come due? They pay — or they struggle to. They don't whine. They don't file manifestos. They certainly don't hire stylists."

The screen flashed a photo of Dr. Graham at a campus lecture — tailored camel polo coat over a navy three-piece suit, glinting cufflinks, leather-bound notebook in hand.

"This is not a man in need," Norrington sneered. "This is a man of means. Of prestige. He owns property. Has a publishing house. Flies to Ghana and France. Has time to wax poetic about Marcus Garvey and thermonuclear racism or whatever flavor-of-the-week theory he's peddling — but when it comes to his debts? Suddenly, it's a political statement."

He slapped the desk.

"Langston Graham isn't oppressed. He's pampered."

The screen cut to a photo of Graham Manor — colonial revival columns, creeping ivy, expansive lawn — with a caption below: "ESTIMATED VALUE: $1.8M"

Norrington pointed.

"You see this? That's not the plantation house of some hedge fund criminal. That's Dr. Graham's residence. Complete with private library, imported mahogany desk, and enough sport coats to outfit a British parliament. He doesn't just wear Brooks Brothers — he curates it. His shoes? Handmade in Northamptonshire, England. The same cobblers that supply European royalty."

He gave a theatrical shrug.

"You know what working-class Americans see when they look at this? Not a freedom fighter. Not a reformer. They see a man who plays professor by day and GQ cover model by night — preaching equity while dodging accountability." He held up a document.

"This is a FOIA-acquired debt record from the Department of Education. Langston Graham owes $142,000. Principal and interest. And it's been sitting for years. He hasn't paid. And don't give me that 'resistance' rhetoric. Rosa Parks didn't skip her bus fare because she wanted to invest in bespoke footwear." A pause. The silence was louder than any applause track.

"This is the new elite defector," Norrington said coldly. "One who hides behind historical grievance to justify personal irresponsibility. This isn't activism. It's arrogance. And America's taxpayers are footing the bill." He fixed his eyes on the camera.

"And I say this not just as a commentator. I say this as someone who paid off his own student loans. Who sat in apartments without heat. Who sent checks home every month. Who didn't wear Oxford cloth and silk ties while dodging the DOE. Langston Graham is not a rebel. He's a refined deadbeat with a Ph.D. in optics." The outro music swelled behind the sound of Norrington's last jab:

"If justice is what he wants, maybe he can start by writing a check."

Chapter 39: The Pushback

The clip went viral by morning. #GrahamDidPay trended on X. So did #NorringtonIsTheProblem. Across the country, educators, activists, former students, and everyday citizens flooded social media with posts defending Dr. Graham — not as a saint, but as a symbol of their own battle.

"This man taught me how to read The Souls of Black Folk in a neighborhood where textbooks were five years out of date. He gave me a future. Now some suit wants to shame him for resisting a predatory system?"

— @JasminEducates, Baltimore

One former student posted a picture of her own diploma beside a worn-out ScholarForge hoodie.

"He paid. Every Saturday. Every lesson plan. Every student he never gave up on."

— @Gracie4Justice

Educators responded with stories: how Dr. Graham donated laptops to students when the district failed, how he covered test fees out-of-pocket, how he stood at school board meetings and challenged budget cuts that targeted Title I programs. Even a quiet post from Dr. Imani Beckett — chair of the sociology department at Smith — gained traction: "When institutions fail, it is the moral responsibility of intellectuals to resist — not to decorate the decay, but to name it. Dr. Graham is not in default. The system is."

Underneath the post, someone added a
photo of Graham reading with children on
the steps of an old church. The caption:
"His wealth is in minds, not mansions."
By evening, the backlash turned political.
Congresswoman Lourdes Enriquez issued
a statement defending Graham by name,
calling Norrington's tirade "textbook
weaponization of class respectability
politics."
But it was the voicemail from his former
dean that struck Langston the most. "You
shook the table, Langston. The right ones
are mad. Stay the course."

Chapter 40: A Rebuttal in Real Time

The livestream began with no fanfare. No intro music. Just Dr. Langston Graham, seated in his study, backlit by bookshelves and a low-glowing banker's lamp. A

pressed oxford shirt, no jacket. A leatherbound notebook open beside him. Calm.
Centered.
"Good evening," he began. "Let me speak plainly."
He paused, letting the quiet stretch.
"This week, a media personality attempted to reduce my resistance to a fashion statement. He claimed I refuse to pay my student loans not out of principle, but out of entitlement. That my wardrobe — soft shouldered suits, and English shoes — disqualifies me from the right to critique systemic injustice."
He folded his hands.
"I'm not going to argue fashion. I've worn secondhand and I've worn bespoke. Neither makes you moral. Neither makes you corrupt. What matters is what you stand for when systems fail the people they were meant to serve." He clicked the remote. A slide appeared: ISAIAH BROWN, Georgia Penitentiary, 1879 – Leased. Died Year 2. Cause: Heatstroke.
"This," he said, gesturing, "is where the system began. Black labor criminalized. Leased to private companies. Used up.

Forgotten. That model never
disappeared — it evolved." Slide two:
Student Loan Debt by Race, 2025 – Black
Borrowers: Avg $52K; Default Rate: 37%
"You want to know why I resist? Because
this debt was never just about dollars. It
was about discipline. Obedience. Because
the moment I made it — legally,
academically, civically — they still found
a chain."
Langston leaned closer.
"When my ancestors were told education
was the ladder out, they climbed it —
barefoot, in borrowed coats, in darkness.
And now that we've reached the rooftop,
they want to repossess the ladder." He
nodded.
"Yes, I could write a check. But I will not
buy silence. Not while students I've taught
are being hunted by interest rates that
outlive their degrees. Not while working
class families carry generational debt just
for daring to dream."
His tone softened but held firm. "This is
not about what I wear. It's about what I
won't wear — and that's a muzzle." He
looked into the lens. "Don't confuse
resistance with irresponsibility. And don't
mistake your comfort with my
compliance. I do not owe you dignity — I
already own it." The stream ended without
applause.
But the silence afterward? It
was full.

Interlude: Smoke Behind the Curtain

The greenroom of American Accountability Tonight was silent, save for the hiss of a sleek espresso machine and the hum of fluorescent lights above. Charles Norrington sat alone, thumbing through his phone with a tight jaw and forced composure. #GrahamDidPay #NorringtonIsTheProblem Langston Graham is not your scapegoat Muzzle This.

He chuckled dryly, scrolling through comment after comment. The likes, the shares, the stitched-together reaction videos. Even the editorial in the Boston Globe calling Dr. Graham's rebuttal "a masterclass in moral clarity."

"Masterclass," he muttered aloud, then tossed the phone on the leather armrest. For a moment, he stared at his own reflection in the dark monitor on the wall — the crisp part in his hair, the navy suit tailored to send messages. But tonight, he looked small inside it. Rattled. A knock came at the door. His producer peeked in. "You've got Congressman Delacroix on line two."

Norrington didn't answer at first. He stood, smoothing his jacket, then walked toward the glass bar cart in the corner and poured himself a finger of scotch. Only then did he pick up the phone.

"Congressman," he said, his voice now oiled and confident. "Loud few. That's all it is."

He listened for a beat.

"No, no — he played it well. I'll give him that. Bookshelves, the sermon cadence, bit of Du Bois for dessert. But he made a mistake."

Another pause.

"He admitted he has the money. Said it plainly. That's all I need." He slipped.

"See, Graham thinks this is still a moral debate. He's playing Frederick Douglass. But we're past that. It's optics now. And in America, perception is policy." The congressman said something that made Norrington smirk.

"Yes, we'll get the committee to open an ethics review. Look into ScholarForge's nonprofit status. Maybe stir the pot about foreign travel. They love that." He set the glass down.

"And I'll write another segment — not angry this time. Calm. Presidential. Frame it as disappointment. Say I expected more of him. Disarm the radicals. Win back the middle."

He looked back at his phone. "And don't worry — by next week, I'll have people asking whether Langston Graham ever even deserved to be called a doctor."

Chapter 41: The Quiet Before...

The grandfather clock in Graham Manor's study ticked like a measured threat. It was nearly midnight, and the house had settled into its familiar hush — but not Langston. He stood by the window, arms crossed, watching shadows bend across the yard like old warnings.

Marcus paced by the fireplace, a rolled-up legal pad in one hand and his hoodie half zipped. His ScholarForge lanyard swung as he moved.

"So now they're talking about subpoenaing ScholarForge's financial records?" he said. "On what grounds? That we raised money for textbooks in Liberia?"

"They'll say the funds were misused," Monroe replied, leaning against the far wall, arms folded, her Oxford blazer still buttoned. "They don't need truth. Just doubt. Just enough to choke the donors."

Langston didn't speak. The digital projector beside his desk hummed as it cycled through screenshots: – An email subject line: Request for Ethics Review

–   A post from a right-wing columnist: Langston Graham — Doctor or Dollar Dodger?

–   A now-viral comment thread debating whether ScholarForge's "influence" was "indoctrination." Marcus stopped pacing. "You said perception becomes policy. What's this become?"

Langston turned. "Punishment."   He
clicked the remote. The next image: a
spreadsheet of ScholarForge alumni.
Names. Test scores. Colleges. Careers.
Lives built from after-school lessons,
Saturday coding camps, ancient texts read
by candlelight.
"They can't undo the truth," Langston
said. "So, they'll try to make the truth
expensive."
Monroe stepped forward. "Then we take
inventory. Staff loyalty. Legal counsel.
Digital security. We leak nothing. We react
to nothing. We document everything."
Marcus looked at them both. "But what
about you?"
Langston raised an eyebrow. Marcus held
firm. "They're going to come for you, not
just the program. They're going to say
you're profiting from pain. That you
turned Black suffering into a platform and
then into property." Langston walked to
the desk, pulled out the leather-bound
journal Monroe had gifted him, and placed
it next to the glowing screen. "I've been
poor. I've been ignored. I've been feared.
Now I'm a threat," he said, voice low but
steady. "So let them come." He opened the
journal to a blank page and wrote two
words at the top: The Reckoning
Then he looked at Marcus. "Tell the
ScholarForge team to begin a curriculum
module on misinformation. We
teach through fire."
"And the donors?" Monroe asked.
Langston smiled. "I'll be meeting with
them. In person. One by one. If they want

a war of appearances, we'll show up undeniable."

Marcus exhaled and nodded. "They tried to cancel you. But they woke the whole classroom."

Chapter 42: The Hearing

The hearing room in the Rayburn House Office Building was colder than it looked on C-SPAN. The walls were paneled in polished wood, the microphones slim and poised like traps. Above the dais, the U.S. flag stood draped behind a brass plaque: HOUSE SUBCOMMITTEE ON FEDERAL LOAN ACCOUNTABILITY AND NONPROFIT COMPLIANCE Langston adjusted his collar. He wore no tie. Just a crisp white shirt beneath a navy blazer, the sleeves rolled one notch at the cuffs — not casual, but deliberate. A quiet refusal of costume. The room buzzed with media and whispered anticipation. Supporters in the back row — teachers, former students, clergy — sat shoulder to shoulder. ScholarForge pins dotted their lapels. A few held signs that wouldn't make it past the cameras: "Debt Is Not Discipline." "Graham Taught Me." "We Are the Return on His Investment." Chairwoman Elaina Delacroix tapped her gavel. "This committee is now in session." She began with procedural framing — the purpose of the inquiry: to determine whether ScholarForge or its founder had violated any laws concerning the use of federal grants, loan forgiveness eligibility, or nonprofit ethics standards. Then came Congressman Bristow, Texas— second-generation oil, first-generation populist.

"Dr. Graham," he began, not looking up from his notes. "Are you currently in default on your federal student loans?" Langston's voice was clear. "According to the Department of Education's records, yes."

"So, you're not denying it?" "I'm confirming it." A murmur rippled. Bristow leaned forward, satisfied. "And do you have the financial means to repay those loans in full today?"

"I do."

"Then let me ask you plainly — what gives you the moral authority to run an educational nonprofit when you, sir, refuse to honor your own educational debt?" Langston didn't flinch.

"The same thing that gave Harriet Tubman the authority to lead — knowing the difference between legality and justice." Gasps. Delacroix banged the gavel. Bristow raised a finger.

"You're no Tubman."

"I'm not," Langston said calmly. "But I do help people escape something — an economic labyrinth masked as opportunity."

Bristow shifted in his chair, eyes narrowing. "You've used ScholarForge to travel abroad, attend private retreats, and speak at engagements. How much of that was taxpayer-funded?"

"Zero," Langston said. "All travel is paid through independent donations or stipends from hosting institutions. My books fund the rest."

"But those books sell because of your public platform," Bristow countered.

"Your brand, sir, is subsidized." Langston opened the leather-bound journal. "Respectfully, Congressman, my brand was built in Newark classrooms with no heat, in borrowed churches, and on Saturday mornings when other men were golfing."

Chairwoman Delacroix interjected, "Let's proceed. Dr. Graham, would you say your decision to withhold repayment is a political act?"

"It's an ethical one," he replied. "Student debt was never just about education. It was about control. And I will not validate a system designed to punish the very mobility it promises."

Another congressman, older, skeptical, chimed in. "And who pays the price for your resistance?"

Langston looked up.

"The same people who always have — but now, they also learn how not to bleed quietly."

There was silence. Even Bristow paused, unsure whether to attack or absorb. From the back row, a young woman stood. Security rushed forward, but she lifted her voice first.

"My name is Janisha Hall," she said. "I was homeless at sixteen. Dr. Graham gave me a place to live and write. Now I'm pre-law at Howard." The room froze.

"He paid me in belief. That debt is paid in full."

The Chairwoman let the silence stretch.

"We thank you for your comment, Miss Hall."

Then she turned back to Graham. "Dr. Graham, the committee will review the evidence and deliberate its findings. But know this — your testimony has been heard."

Langston nodded, collected his notebook, and stood.

And as he walked out of the chamber, cufflinks glinting beneath rolled sleeves, the echo of Janisha's voice walked with him — louder than any gavel.

Chapter 43: The Manor at Midnight

It was nearly 2:00 a.m. in the quiet suburb of Silver Creek, just outside Washington, D.C. The porch lights of Graham Manor had finally gone dark, save for one in the study window — a faint amber glow spilling across the trimmed hedges and flagstone path.

The press vans had long rolled away. But the air still carried a scent of tension — like the aftermath of a thunderstorm.

Inside, Langston sat alone in his study. The windows were cracked open, letting in the soft rustle of elm trees. He hadn't moved in an hour. His collar was loosened, sleeves rolled, a glass of untouched bourbon beside his journal. The hearing played again in his mind: the smug drawl of Congressman Bristow, the sharp clang of the gavel, the tremble in Janisha Hall's voice when she rose from the back row.

Monroe entered without knocking.

She wore slippers now, and one of Langston's oversized ScholarForge hoodies — an unlikely pairing with her usual Oxbridge poise, though the fire in her eyes remained.

"You didn't dodge a single question," she said quietly. "You knew they'd come with knives."

Langston didn't look up. "I'm not afraid to bleed."

"That's not bravery," she said, crossing the room, "that's martyrdom in tweed." He turned toward her. "You disapprove?" "I disagree," Monroe replied, taking a seat across from him. "You think suffering authenticates the message. But sometimes the message needs to survive, not burn at the stake."

Langston poured another drink, this time offering her a glass. She took it. "You think I should've paid?" he asked. "I think," she said carefully, "that you've already paid in ways they'll never comprehend. But this—" she gestured toward the leather journal, then toward the glowing screen still paused on a C-SPAN frame "—this is no longer personal protest. It's political ammunition. You've become the battlefield." Langston closed the journal. "They're trying to turn ScholarForge into collateral," he said. "If I back down now, every teacher who dared to resist — every student who found their voice — gets labeled reckless by association." Monroe's voice softened. "I know. But you need to be precise now. Not poetic." She leaned forward. "This isn't about dignity anymore, Langston. This is about leverage. And they're not just aiming for your reputation. They're angling for your funding, your access, your legacy." He looked into the fire. "And I won't let them turn that into ash." A long pause stretched between them. Then Monroe said, barely above a whisper, "The system knows how to kill an idea, Langston — it starts by making the visionary look irresponsible." Langston finally met her eyes. "Then we build a vision that refuses to die.”

Chapter 44: The Orchard Revisited

The morning after the hearing, a black car waited at the edge of Graham Manor's long drive. No license plate. No markings. Just tinted windows and a low, deliberate hum — the kind of sound engineered for discretion, not drama.
Langston opened the passenger door and slid in.
Inside sat a man dressed like no one else in Washington: a signature deep purple blazer, mandarin collar beneath, crisp white tee, polished ankle boots, and silver rimmed glasses that reflected light like precision tools.
Langston smirked as he closed the door. "Obadiah... you're still wearing that purple blazer?"
Obadiah Fountain, as composed as ever, replied without looking up from his tablet. "Yes. Always."
Langston shook his head, already laughing. "Man, remember that time we were on the yard at Howard, and those young brothers thought you were a Bruh?"
Obadiah finally cracked a grin, the rare kind that revealed both his teeth and his age. "They started hopping in my direction and throwing up the hooks like I owed them line dues."
They both rolled with laughter — the kind that collapses the weight of years into one moment of shared absurdity. "They were so serious," Langston wheezed. "One of them said, 'That's Big

Bruh from '79.'"

Obadiah nodded, chuckling. "And I said, 'Nah, brother. I pledged Thermodynamics.'"

Langston wiped his eyes. "You never told them the truth, either." "I didn't have to," Obadiah said. "The blazer handled that."

The car eased onto the boulevard, heading east toward Union Station. Their laughter faded into the quiet of two men who had once slept in cinder block dorms and now moved markets.

They had first met twenty-one years earlier, at The Orchard — a converted peach farm outside Summerton, South Carolina. Obadiah had transformed it into a solar-powered research sanctuary: part greenhouse, part think tank, part intellectual dojo.

Langston had arrived with a duffel bag, a fellowship he couldn't cash, and a head full of Baldwin and bell hooks. Obadiah had greeted him not with a handshake, but a question:

"You believe the mind is the final frontier?"

Langston had replied,

"No. I believe it's the last plantation."

Obadiah had smiled for the first time in weeks.

It was there that ThermaBlack was born — a black polymer-enhanced chemical compound that, when mixed with tar or asphalt, made roads, pipelines, and even rooftops resistant to freezing. It performed with radical efficiency in subzero conditions, reducing maintenance costs by up to 78% and saving lives in regions where winter was a weapon. Obadiah didn't sell it. He licensed it — to nations. From Finland to South Korea, from Kenya to Iceland, ThermaBlack was quietly transforming infrastructure under sovereign agreements that guaranteed local manufacturing and job creation. By the time he turned 52, Dr. Fountain was a multimillionaire, with no corporate board to answer to and no ambition to be a household name.

"I didn't invent it to get rich," he once told Langston. "I invented it because my mother had to melt snow on a Coleman stove just to flush a toilet. Wealth means nothing if it doesn't bend gravity in someone else's direction." Now, back in the car, Fountain reached beneath the seat and pulled out a leather portfolio.

He slid it to Langston.

"Open it."

Langston did. Inside: a signed licensing agreement granting ScholarForge Urban Labs exclusive U.S. infrastructure rights to deploy ThermaBlack in public school systems, underserved communities, and federal urban development zones.

Langston stared at the figures. "This is... this is power."

"Correct," Obadiah said. "Structured. Legal. Unapologetic."

"You're bringing ScholarForge into the international game."

"I'm anchoring you in something they can't smear."

Langston closed the portfolio. "Why now?"

Obadiah looked out the window at the Capitol dome in the distance. "Because I watched them drag your name across congressional marble like a rogue invoice. And I remembered how we once rewired flood sensors in a barn with $13 between us and three feet of swamp. I remembered that your mind — not your checkbook — is the real threat." Langston nodded, but hesitated.

"This puts you in their sights, too."

Obadiah adjusted the lapel of his unmistakable blazer. "Langston, I license inventions to presidents. I am already in their sights."

A pause. Then a half-smile. "I wear purple, so they never mistake me for their servant."

Chapter 45: The Black Futures Summit

They called it The Summit, but it felt more like a reckoning.
Held in a glass-domed conference hall overlooking the Anacostia River, the Black Futures Summit had become the unofficial Davos for global Black excellence. No red carpets. No celebrity panels. Just minds, money, and mission — in equal measure.
The audience was standing-room only: founders, diplomats, scholars, engineers, educators, and billion-dollar fund managers in Kente-lined suits and Jordan IVs, in dashikis paired with digital wearables.
It was day three when the whispers began.
Langston Graham was here.
Obadiah Fountain too.
They were about to speak — together. No one had seen them together in public for years. Not since the ScholarForge pilot programs had made quiet ripples. Now, with controversy at Langston's heels and Obadiah's global reach untouched, the air hummed with the anticipation of tectonic movement.
The lights dimmed.
The moderator, a Kenyan-born venture capitalist named Chiamaka Douglass, took the mic.
"Our next segment is not a panel. It's a proposal. A challenge. A line in the sand."
She stepped aside.

Langston took the stage first — navy suit, open collar, no notes. His presence, even after the bruising hearing, felt sharper than ever. Not wounded — refined. He didn't start with his résumé. He started with the truth.

"They said I defaulted. But what they didn't say was why.

I refused to pay into a system that feeds off the dream of the poor. I refused to buy silence at the cost of complicity." The screen behind him shifted — images of overcrowded classrooms, cracked sidewalks, shivering students in broken trailers labeled "temporary" for decades.

"If roads can freeze, so can opportunity. If pipes can burst, so can hope. That's why ScholarForge is expanding — not just curriculum, but infrastructure. Not just classrooms — ecosystems." He paused. Then turned to the side. "And for that, I needed a different kind of partner." Dr. Fountain entered in silence — regal, centered, and unmistakable in his signature purple blazer, a thermochromic pin on the lapel that changed color with body heat. He carried no slides. He carried the room.

"Ladies and gentlemen," Obadiah began, "I invented ThermaBlack because the world kept making winters longer for the poor. I refused to let geography decide survival. Today, I'm licensing my technology to ScholarForge Urban Labs — not as charity. Not as optics. But as alignment."

The screen shifted again. This time:
ThermaBlack + ScholarForge Urban Labs
→ Target Launch Cities: Detroit, Newark, Baton Rouge, Birmingham, Flint.
Langston stepped beside him. "We're building the first generation of public schools in America designed by us, for us, with infrastructure engineered for Black futures — from the parking lot to the principal's office." Gasps.
Then cheers.
Fountain lifted the mic one last time.
"We don't just want equity," he said.
"We're issuing patents on it." The applause rose. From the back rows to the front. From old heads to Gen Z crypto founders. From Nigerian diplomats to North Philly principals. Because this wasn't a speech. It was a declaration of intent.

Chapter 46: The Weight of the Crest

The morning paper sat folded on Langston's front step, the headline in bold, all-caps: "Questions Surround ScholarForge Founder's Family Military Record" Langston didn't pick it up. He already knew what it said. What it meant. The timing wasn't a coincidence. The wording wasn't accidental. The attack had shifted—from strategy to ancestry. Inside, Rev. Dr. Malachi Mitchell stood at the bay window, one hand in his coat pocket, the other resting lightly on the spine of a leather Bible worn soft from decades of funerals, marches, and firestorms. His gaze lingered on the magnolia tree outside, bare-limbed and brittle in the early morning chill. "You're bleeding legacy now," the reverend said quietly. Langston leaned against the kitchen island, arms folded across his chest. He hadn't slept. He looked like a man who'd walked through fire and made it out—smoldering, not unscathed.

"They want the story to be that I came from shadows," he muttered. Malachi turned slowly, his eyes neither pitying nor harsh. Just clear. "Maybe you did," he said. "But the job of a Graham has never been to run from the shadows. It's to walk through them upright. Head high. Spine steady." He stepped over, placed the Bible on the counter beside Langston, and held his gaze.

"You bear a name built with broken hands. You carry a mind sharpened by rooms that never wanted you in them. What you cannot do, son—what you must not do—is gather mud on your escutcheon." Langston blinked. The phrase caught him off guard. "Escutcheon?" he repeated softly. "I haven't heard that since Patty Crocker used to whisper it when I came home from school… covered in dirt and bruises." Malachi nodded slowly. "Because she knew."

He placed a hand on Langston's shoulder. It was the kind of gesture that meant I know your whole bloodline. I'm not impressed—I'm invested. "An escutcheon isn't just about family," he said. "It's about public witness. About what you carry in front of people who are waiting to call you counterfeit. It's the shield you polish not for vanity, but for the ones who come after."

Langston glanced down at the smooth oak of the counter. It bore faint grooves— marks from past meals, late-night planning sessions, quiet arguments with Monroe, strategy meetings with ScholarForge fellows. The surface told its own story. "I'm holding the shield steady, Reverend," he said, voice lower now. "But they already threw the mud. They've got talking heads spinning lies about my father. About Korea. About stolen valor.

They're framing my family like we forged our way into dignity."

Malachi's expression didn't change. He listened like a man who'd been accused more times than he could count—and was still standing.

"That's because they know your name rings louder than their scandal," he said. "They don't come for you when you're small. They come when you're too steady to move, too loud to ignore." Langston exhaled. "This was never about my record. Or my father's. It's about the idea of me. The idea of a man like me daring to speak with authority in spaces they think belong to them." Malachi nodded once.

"Exactly."

He tapped the cover of the Bible once with a knuckle.

"They didn't crucify Jesus for feeding people. They crucified Him because He wouldn't apologize for who sent Him." Langston looked up, something like grief flickering across his face. Or maybe it was clarity.

"And what about you, Reverend?" he asked. "What kept you steady when they came for your name?"

Malachi's answer was quiet. "Knowing I didn't carry it alone."

The two men stood there a moment longer, suspended in the morning stillness.

Outside, the first breeze of spring teased the magnolia tree.

Langston finally walked to the front door. He looked down at the folded newspaper,

the bold headline still visible through the plastic sleeve. Then he reached down and picked it up—not to read it, but to own it. As he closed the door behind him, he spoke without turning back:
"Let them write what they want. My name was forged long before they learned to spell it."
Malachi smiled. Not broadly, but enough.
"The world doesn't fear a name with wealth, Langston. It fears a name with weight."

Chapter 47: The Ink Remembers

The world had shouted all week. Headlines screamed. Commentators foamed. Allies scrambled. Enemies sharpened their phrases like knives at a banquet.

But here, in the quiet sanctuary of his study, Dr. Langston Elkanah Graham let the silence reclaim its authority. He had turned off the lights except for the green glass banker's lamp that cast a circle of golden warmth on the oak desk. The windows were open just enough to let in the evening's hush — the occasional rustle of leaves, the hum of cicadas, the distant clap of train wheels slicing through suburban stillness.

On the desk lay two companions older than his doctorate: – A Moroccan leather journal, handstitched with gold filigree threading the edges, the texture worn smooth where his thumb always landed. It smelled faintly of sandalwood and age. He bought it from a third-generation craftsman in Fez who had no website, no business card — just a name etched into a block of olivewood and a quiet mastery that told Langston he was in sacred company. – And beside it, his most intimate instrument: the Montegrappa Extra 1930, a fountain pen passed down to him from a professor who once told him, "Every movement of this nib is an act of self-respect." The pen had a weight to it — not heavy, but definite — like a promise kept. Langston cracked the spine of the journal open and ran his fingers along the grain of the paper. He didn't journal for posterity.

He journaled because the world demanded reaction, and he needed reflection. It was a way to remember himself before others misnamed him.

He clicked the pen's cap loose and let the ink begin.

May 14 – 11:47 PM

They've pulled the thread on the one thing I never unraveled — my father.

A dishonorable discharge wrapped in "honorable conditions." Children scattered across states like postmarks on a life never mailed home.

And now, they're laying it at my feet.

Let them.

If they believe my father's complexity discredits my clarity, they've never read Baldwin.

Still, I feel the old voice in me — the one that wants to correct every narrative. That wants to shout dates, documents, the context they conveniently cropped out.

But I will not lower myself to their volume.

I will write instead.

He paused and sipped the glass of room temperature scotch that sat untouched since the last paragraph. The fire in it didn't comfort him. It confirmed him.

Problem: How do I protect the mission without erasing myself?

ScholarForge was never about me — but it was never not about me, either. Every lesson, every lunchroom discussion, every book we placed in a child's hand carried my fingerprints. Answer: I frame myself not as the architect, but as the cornerstone. Built upon, not centered. And the cornerstone doesn't shout. It holds.
Let the truth speak in full sentences. Let the facts be crafted — not fired. He turned to a fresh page. The words came slower now, but steadier. Reframe. Reset. Reassert. Let me not defend what I do but declare what we are. ScholarForge is not a brand. It is a resistance curriculum.
Not just a response to educational inequity — it is a strategy of freedom infrastructure.
I do not owe America silence about her scaffolding.
I owe my students clarity about their inheritance.
He stopped writing. Closed the journal.
And for the first time all week, he smiled.
The words weren't armor.
They were instruction.

Chapter 48: The Letter

Posted to ScholarForge.org, 9:17 a.m. Shared via public livestream and letter to donors.
Title: On Inheritance and Intention by Dr. Langston E. Graham, I have always believed that names carry weight — not just because of what they mean, but because of what they endure. My name has endured accusations, headlines, algorithms, and now, a strategic campaign to separate my history from my humanity. I was not born from perfection. I was born from perseverance.
I carry the blood of a man who fought his way out of the silence that the military assigned him, and a woman who prayed books into our living room like they were groceries.
If you believe that a man is discredited by his father's past, then you haven't met our students.
If you believe a school is invalidated by the complexity of its founder, then you don't understand liberation.
I will not answer in anger.
I will answer with structure. ScholarForge was built from Saturday mornings and whispered Hebrew in borrowed classrooms. It was built from the mouths of 12-year-olds learning to quote Octavia Butler. It was built from my own grandmother's hands, who ironed shirts

and expectations with equal fire. What we
teach is not just literature, math, or history.
We teach intention — how to build a
future and not apologize for surviving the
past.
To those watching — waiting for a
retraction or a retreat:
We are not retreating. We are retooling.
And to every young person reading this:
You are not the sum of what they've
withheld from you.
You are the spark that names the storm.
Let them write what they want. You write
what's next.

Chapter 49: The Ashes of Elegance

The room was dim, the only light spilling from the projector screen behind Dr. Langston Graham. The image seared across it showed the charred remains of the Nottoway Plantation—its once-grand white columns now blackened, its famed rotunda cracked and smoking, sagging under the weight of history it had long tried to hide.

Langston stood at the front of the ScholarForge Lecture Hall. The silence in the room wasn't fear. It was reverence. Because everyone in the room could feel it: something old had died, and something new might yet be born. He cleared his throat. "This," he said, gesturing toward the image, "is Nottoway. Burned. Not in 1865. Not during the Civil Rights Movement. Not by storm or siege. But yesterday."

He paused, letting the gravity sink in. "The news called it a tragedy. 'A loss for the state of Louisiana.' A symbol of Southern charm, history, luxury—gone in smoke. But let me ask you something…"

He clicked the remote. A new image flickered on the screen: a yellowed photograph of enslaved people on the grounds of Nottoway in the 1860s. "Did anyone mourn them?"

The students shifted in their seats. "I don't celebrate fire. I don't take joy in destruction. But I recognize what fire reveals. Sometimes it shows us what was already rotting. Sometimes, the flame just tells the truth faster than the museum tour ever will."

He clicked again. A photo of the current resort: manicured lawns, wine glasses on white tablecloths under the shade of oak trees that once covered slave cabins. "I've walked past gift shops built on slave quarters. Watched weddings staged in rooms where women were whipped into silence. I've seen the erasure painted over with mint juleps and string quartets." Another pause. Then, with the calm clarity of a professor who knew both the wound and the remedy, Langston continued: "We are being taught to mourn architecture but not ancestors. To fund preservation but not reparations. To see fire as tragedy when it touches brick, but not when it's been burning in our blood for centuries." A student in the back—one of the newer ScholarForge fellows—raised his hand. "So… are you saying it's good that it burned?"

Langston nodded slowly, not in agreement, but in understanding. "No. I'm saying the fire didn't start yesterday. It started in 1859, when Nottoway was built on backs instead of foundations. It's been smoldering ever since." He stepped closer to the podium and placed a leather-bound journal beside the laptop.

"This fire is a metaphor," he said. "But it's also a message. That no matter how polished the story, truth still has a way of demanding to be told."

Chapter 50: The Quiet Before the Forge

The morning after the letter was posted, Langston Graham stood alone in the lecture hall at ScholarForge. The chairs were still warm from the bodies of last night's emergency meeting, the air still heavy with questions he hadn't answered—and didn't need to. Not yet. The sun broke in like it was reclaiming something—not just the room, but the resolve.

He moved slowly, tracing the edges of the podium with his fingers. The same podium where once, before the headlines and hearings, he taught a lesson on Baldwin and belonging. He remembered the students who stayed behind afterward to argue, to cry, to ask how someone like them could write something that reached so far into the future. He remembered a girl named Zara who'd whispered, "Sir, I didn't know we were allowed to say things like that."

Now, she was at Howard, majoring in philosophy.

The door creaked open. Monroe entered, silent at first, then placed a thick envelope on the desk.

"Final report. The audit's closed," she said, eyes narrowing. "They didn't find what they wanted."

Langston gave a wry smile. "They never do when the truth doesn't fit the narrative."

He glanced at the envelope but didn't open it. What was in it no longer mattered. It had never really been about money. It had been about momentum—about control. If they could pause ScholarForge long enough, freeze its credibility mid-step, maybe the students would hesitate. Maybe the donors would shrink. Maybe the next generation would settle for the lie.

But that didn't happen.

The livestream of The Letter had reached 3.1 million views overnight. Students around the country had stitched their own stories into the thread—photos of libraries they built in barbershops, tutoring sessions in laundromats, lessons on resistance carved into chalkboards and church basements. ScholarForge had become more than a place. It had become a posture.

A statement.

A refusal.

He walked through the empty halls—past photos of the inaugural ScholarForge cohort, past the timeline mural painted by students: from the Black Panthers' free breakfast program to the Maroon societies to the coded songs of Harriet Tubman's map. Education as inheritance. Knowledge as insurgency.

As he turned the corner to his office, Langston paused.

A framed photograph caught his eye—one he'd passed a thousand times but now looked different.

It was Grandma Patty Crocker. Smiling.

Apron still on. Holding a leatherbound Bible in one hand and a composition notebook in the other.

The caption below it read:

"There is no such thing as wasted wisdom. Just wisdom that hasn't been planted yet."

Langston blinked, then chuckled quietly to himself.

She had been the first forge.

Before ScholarForge was even a thought, Patty Crocker was teaching theology and long division at her kitchen table—while biscuits browned in the oven and soap operas hummed from the living room. She taught discipline by example and scripture by lived experience. She prayed over multiplication tables and ironed her grandson's shirt like she was flattening his future into shape.

She was the one who handed him his first journal and said, "Write it down. The world forgets our stories too easily." She never made it past the eighth grade, but her mind could cut through doctrine and deception alike. And when the world tried to convince Langston that brilliance needed a pedigree, it was her voice that reminded him: *We were brilliant before they started keeping records.* He entered his office.

On the desk was a new journal—leatherbound, of course. The same kind Monroe still bought for him when they travelled to Fez. This one was embossed with a new inscription:

Still Here. Still Building.

He sat, uncapped his pen, and wrote:

May 18.
The storm passed. Or maybe we just learned to walk through it upright. ScholarForge was never a shield. It was a forge. That means it takes heat, hammers, and friction to shape anything worth keeping.

I have made peace with the fact that they may never understand what we're building here. It was never for them anyway. This is for the Zakaris and Zoes. For the ones they almost forgot.

And for Grandma Patty, whose prayers are still scaffolding every wall we raise. There was a knock on the door. He looked up. It was Marcus—tie loose, backpack slung, breathless. "They're ready," he said.

"Who?" Langston asked.

"The students. They organized a teach-in. Hundreds in the gym. They want you to open it."

Langston nodded slowly and stood. "Then let's begin."

As he walked toward the gym, the sounds grew louder—not angry, but alive. Not a protest. A proclamation. ScholarForge banners had been unfurled. Chalk messages lined the concrete walkways: Liberation has a lesson plan.

We are the curriculum now. This isn't an ending. It's a syllabus. He took the stage with no notes. Just breath. Just presence.

He looked out at the sea of faces—old and young, tired and fierce. Some students wore robes—they would graduate next month. Others were still in middle school.

But all of them, Langston realized, were
already authors of the world to come.
He adjusted the mic. Cleared his throat.
Then said simply:
"We didn't just survive the storm.
We designed in it.
And now, we're rebuilding in public. Not
with permission.
But with purpose."
Applause thundered. But Langston didn't
move.
He waited for the silence again.
It arrived—not empty, but full of weight.
And in that silence, something new
began. Not a rebrand. Not a rebuttal.
A renaissance.

Chapter 51: The Rewriting

The velvet hush of the Atlas Club was thick with memory.

Langston Graham sat beneath the golden dome of the library room—a private sanctuary within the Club—surrounded by portraits of men who had dared to remember when the nation preferred forgetting. The room was paneled in dark walnut, lined with glass-encased first editions, and softly lit by a brass chandelier that seemed to hum with the weight of unwritten speeches. Above the fireplace hung the portrait of Kevin Greene, the Club's founder—a visionary who'd once said, "If they won't teach our story, we'll build a place where it lives in every chair." The Atlas Club was Greene's answer to erasure. And tonight, it was Langston's refuge from heartbreak.

The cigar in Langston's hand was Cuban—rolled in Havana, aged in cedar, selected with care by Greene's surviving nephew, now the club's sommelier. Langston had taken just three pulls, slow and intentional, letting the earthy warmth and sweetness settle deep in his chest. He wasn't here for its taste. He was here for its ritual.

He leaned back in the oxblood leather armchair that had long since adjusted to the curve of his shoulders. The air was thick with the scent of sandalwood, old paper, and single malt. His legs crossed neatly at the ankle. The fire crackled with perfect rhythm.

But the silence inside him was not peace. It was grief.

Pie. What he calls his granddaughter. The light in his days. The future in his hands. She had asked him a question that wrecked him more than any panel, any accusation, any raid or headline ever had: "Pawpaw… if they already did this to people a long time ago, why are they doing it again?"

The question had been asked over pancakes. With syrup on her cheek. With innocence that didn't yet understand what kind of world needed to ask such things twice.

And he had no good answer. Not then. Now, with the weight of the firelight and the ghost of history thick around him, he tried.

Langston reached into the inside pocket of his camel blazer and withdrew a thick envelope. The ScholarForge crest was embossed in gold on the flap. Inside was a half-written letter—the first few lines scratched out and rewritten over and over in his tight, deliberate script.

He uncapped his Montblanc pen, steadied his hand, and began again.

"Pie," he wrote,

"When you grow older, you'll read about the 19th and 20th centuries. You'll see photographs in sepia and black-and white—lynchings, marches, fire hoses, segregated water fountains, book burnings, closed schools, censored voices. You'll read of injustices that were so plain, so loud, that you'll believe—surely—we had learned."

His hand paused. The clock ticked in syncopated time.

"But history doesn't always teach. Sometimes it repeats. Sometimes it hides in new words, new policies, new silences. And sometimes—God help us—it's repackaged in the language of freedom."

Langston glanced up. A few men were talking quietly at the bourbon bar. One of them nodded in his direction. Another sipped and kept his eyes down. Everyone knew what was happening in the country. ScholarForge had become a symbol—not just of education, but of resistance.

And resistance was dangerous again.

He kept writing.

"What they used to call 'Jim Crow,' they now call 'school choice.' What was once 'mass incarceration' is now 'zero tolerance.' What was once redlining is now zoning. What was once banning Black history is now a call to protect the 'integrity of the curriculum.' They've learned to use softer words for the same hard truths." He exhaled.

"You will be told it's different. That this is progress. That your memory is the problem. But don't let them fool you. You come from people who carried memory like a weapon. Who turned basements into classrooms and whispers into witness."

Langston sat the cigar down gently in the ashtray. It burned evenly, quietly, like a clock marking time.

He looked toward the shelves—books by Du Bois, Baldwin, Morrison, Crummell, and Clarke. Spines straight. Stories still breathing.

"They silenced our teachers, so we taught each other. They closed our schools, so we opened churches. They outlawed our languages, so we wrote new ones. We survived erasure with elegance. And now they are trying again." He took a sip of scotch—peaty, aged, bitter at first, then smooth. "Pie, I am sorry you must learn this. I am sorry that the same ink used to write justice is now being used to redact it. But I will not let you inherit silence. That is not your birthright."

His hand trembled slightly as he neared the end.

"You carry a name that endured. Carry it with defiance. Carry it with grace. And when the world tries to convince you, this is the first time—

—you look them in the eye and say: No. My grandfather told me the truth." He placed the pen down, folded the letter, and sealed the envelope with a ScholarForge wax stamp. Then he wrote in strong block letters:

FOR PIE. OPEN WHEN THEY TRY TO ERASE US AGAIN.

Langston stood slowly, cigar in hand, and walked the letter to the fireplace. He didn't burn it. He placed it behind Kevin Greene's portrait—in the hidden panel that only members of the board knew existed. The place where real stories were kept, when the world became too dangerous for

truth to live in plain sight. He stepped
back, took a final draw of his cigar, and
whispered—not a prayer, but a promise.
"They may rewrite history." "But we will
rewrite legacy." Then he exhaled.
And the smoke rose, like memory made
visible, curling toward the ceiling like the
names of ancestors still watching.

Chapter 52: Mirrors That Never Lie

The clink of ice in cut-crystal glasses was the only sound between them for several minutes. The Atlas Club—quiet tonight—offered its usual blend of old money and hush-hush strategy. A bastion nestled in a D.C. suburb, where leather-bound books lined the walls and the weight of tradition could be felt in every polished surface. It was the kind of place where history didn't just hang—it loomed.

Langston Graham sat beneath a framed lithograph of the Emancipation Proclamation, sipping slowly from a glass of neat bourbon. Across from him, Obadiah Fountain swirled a glass of Bordeaux with slow deliberation. His purple blazer, now draped behind his chair, caught the glow of the chandelier above them.

"This place still smells like entitled nostalgia," Obadiah muttered, his voice low and sharp. "All this mahogany and marble and they think it makes the lies look noble."

Langston didn't answer immediately. His gaze lingered on a nearby display case— an original copy of the 1965 Voting Rights Act, encased like a relic. A museum piece. A warning.

"I've come to believe," Langston said at last, "that the government thinks we've

either forgotten… or never really knew."
Obadiah nodded, leaning forward.
"They're banking on it. Generational
amnesia. Institutional gaslighting. They
assume our students won't ask questions.
That our silence means agreement. Or
worse—ignorance."

Langston shook his head slowly. "They
dismantle civil rights protections, abolish
DEI, and repackage it as administrative
streamlining. They toss around words like
'efficiency' and 'colorblindness' as if
justice were a budgeting issue."

Obadiah scoffed. "The unmitigated gall…
asking us to trust them while they
disassemble the very protections we bled
to win. As if they've earned our
confidence with centuries of deceit."

He paused, eyes narrowing. "You
remember *The Remains of the Day*?"

Langston gave a slight nod. "Kazuo
Ishiguro. Brilliant. Devastating."

Obadiah leaned in, his voice quiet but
heavy. "There's this moment. Stevens—
the butler—realizes he spent his life
serving a man who was morally bankrupt.
He was *duped*. Loyal to a fault. Polished.
Obedient. Blind."

Langston exhaled sharply. "And when he
finally sees the truth, all he has left are the
remains of the day."

Obadiah stared at his wine. "That's what they want from us, Langston. To serve quietly. To teach diluted history. To cut the legs off truth in the name of neutrality. They want us to reach the end of our careers, full of regret, asking ourselves: *Was I duped?*"

Langston's voice cut in, low and pointed. "But we are *not* Stevens. We are *not* silent servants to empires that pretend to forget their sins."

"They fear that," Obadiah murmured. "That we remember. That we *teach* others to remember. That we've read the footnotes, traced the policies back to their shadows, and dared to speak the parts they hoped would rot in archives."

"They thought DEI was a gift," Langston added. "It was never that. It was a reckoning. A foot in the door we weren't supposed to walk through."

Obadiah nodded. "And now they're trying to slam it shut. But they're too late. We're already in the room. Already building."

Langston glanced toward the high shelves. "They call resistance divisive. But what's more divisive than pretending history never happened?"

Obadiah finished his wine, placed the glass down with a quiet finality. "They want the narrative back in their hands. But we've digitized it. Buried it in curriculum. Fiction. Code. Our work's been seeded in the very minds they forgot to monitor." Langston stood, sliding his chair back with a soft scrape. "We've seen this before. Jim Crow in khakis. Redlining in policy briefs. Intimidation behind administrative smiles."

Obadiah rose beside him. "And we answer the same way—through memory. Through unyielding truth."

The chandelier flickered slightly as the room settled again. A senator across the room tapped a tablet without looking up.

Langston straightened his collar. "I'd rather die standing in defiance than live duped by decorum."

Obadiah smiled grimly. "History may repeat, Langston. But this time, it remembers our names."

They left the club together, two scholars in the night. Not relics. Not footnotes. But the authors of a living resistance.

And this time, they weren't leaving behind the remains of the day.

They were preparing for the rising of the next.

Chapter 53: The Park Bench Doctrine

The air was sharp with early spring. The cherry blossoms along Constitution Avenue were just beginning to shed, their petals dancing like soft confetti on the breeze. Dr. Langston Elkanah Graham walked slowly, his polished oxfords crunching the gravel along the National Mall. Beside him was Marcus Baker, notebook in hand, eyes scanning the horizon.

They stopped before a low bench just outside Lafayette Park—no plaque, no pedestal, just timeworn wood, smoothed by decades of silent thought.

Langston tapped the backrest. "This is where Bernard Baruch used to sit."

Marcus tilted his head. "Who?"

Langston chuckled. "Of course you haven't heard of him. Baruch was a millionaire who actually served the people. He made his money on Wall Street, then spent the rest of his life, giving presidents advice—from Wilson to Truman."

Marcus raised an eyebrow. "Sounds like a unicorn."

"He was. Jewish. Southern born. A man of wealth who believed wisdom was for sharing, not hoarding. They called this spot *Baruch's Bench*. He didn't need a title—his counsel was his legacy." Marcus jotted notes in his leather-bound journal.

Langston gazed toward the White House, half-shrouded in security and silence. "Baruch had a saying I've never forgotten. He said, '*Don't try to buy at the bottom and sell at the top. It can't be done except by liars.*'"

Marcus paused mid-scribble. "So... don't believe the hype?"

Langston nodded. "Exactly. The student loan system? It's built on that lie. They told your generation: *borrow at the bottom, climb to the top.* But they never told you the ladder was made of debt and delay. No safety net. No forgiveness. Just compounding interest in a rigged economy."

They sat on the bench together. For a moment, neither spoke.

Then Langston leaned forward.

"You ever wonder why the Department of Education was created in the first place?"

"To help people?"

Langston smiled grimly. "To protect them. From exploitation. From private interests that turned schools into factories and students into collateral. But now they're dismantling that, piece by piece."

Memory Insert — 1946, New York

In the shadow of a midtown office, Bernard Baruch stood before a chalkboard, sleeves rolled up, flanked by two young men in military uniforms just returned from the war.

"You've seen what unchecked power can do," he told them, drawing a circle and a line through its center. "But this—this is a balance sheet. Not a battlefield. Remember this: *markets run on confidence but survive on integrity.* Never lie to people about what you're offering. If you can't explain it, you shouldn't sell it."

One of the men raised a hand. "But sir, don't they say buy low and sell high?"

Baruch turned sharply.

"Don't try to buy at the bottom and sell at the top. It can't be done except by liars."

He paused, letting the words fall like gavel strokes.

"Better to earn slow and sleep well."

Back to Present Day – ScholarForge Seminar

The classroom was buzzing. The walls of ScholarForge's DC annex were plastered with clippings from economic history: the

GI Bill, the 2008 crash, and a framed reproduction of the Baruch Plan.

Langston stood before a dry-erase board, arms crossed.

"Today's prompt: *Is student debt a market failure or a moral failure?* Defend your stance using precedent."

Marcus stood at the podium. "It's both. And the precedent is Bernard Baruch. He used his knowledge of finance to serve the public good, not to entrap people in debt. When markets punish people for being poor—when they sell you a future in exchange for your dignity—it's no longer economics. It's exploitation."

A student in the back raised their hand. "But isn't that just capitalism?"

Langston stepped in.

"No. That's predatory capitalism. Baruch didn't confuse greed with genius. He warned against it. He understood that power without ethics is just legalized theft."

He gestured toward the class.
"You're not here just to decode systems. You're here to redesign them."

Later that night, as Langston returned to the bench, he found a small, laminated card tucked between the slats. In Marcus's neat handwriting, it read:

"Don't try to buy at the bottom and sell at the top. It can't be done except by liars."

— Bernard Baruch

Langston smiled.

A bench. A doctrine. A new generation.

The resurrection had already begun.

Chapter 54: The Gilded Threshold

The rain had just begun, faint and misty against the high windows of Dr. Langston Graham's private study. Monroe had returned from the ScholarForge Annex, her trench coat damp, a box of recovered books in her arms.

Langston took them gently, brushing the top volume with reverence. "These were in the storage crates?"

"Hidden behind a row of outdated tax codes. Someone didn't want them seen," Monroe said, eyeing the cracked spine of a familiar title.

Langston lifted it: *The Philadelphian*, first edition. Worn cloth cover, gold leaf nearly faded. He opened it. Inside, in slanted cursive: *To Patty Crocker – For when the gates seem sealed shut. —N.L., 1960*

He raised an eyebrow. "N.L. That's Nelson Langford. A friend of my grandmother's from the old days. He must've given this to her not long after she started keeping those clippings for me— back when I first started asking questions about legacy and law."

Monroe peered over his shoulder. "I remember this novel. About a man who becomes a top lawyer in Philadelphia and challenges the social clubs and old bloodlines."

Langston nodded. "It was Powell's quiet critique of America's invisible aristocracy."

He flipped to a dog-eared page. Patty had underlined the line:

"A Philadelphian is not a man who lives in Philadelphia. He is a man whose grandmother lived in Philadelphia."

Langston let the words sit there between them.

"She loved that line," he said. "Because it wasn't just about cities—it was about lineage. That's how they keep us out, Monroe. Not with law, but with legacy."

He closed the book briefly, then opened it again with more urgency.

"They don't have to say it. They just look at you in a certain way, and you know."

"She wrote in the margin," he said, pointing.

In Patty's steady handwriting: *That's how the superintendent looked at me in 1961. After he read my last name.* Monroe exhaled. "We know that look."

Langston stared ahead, voice steady. "Marcus knows it too. After the fellowship interview. They shook his hand, smiled politely. But he said he could feel the no before they spoke it."

"Because respectability doesn't erase memory," Monroe said. "Not theirs. Not ours."

Langston stood and walked toward the fireplace. The framed photograph of his grandmother stared down—stoic, elegant, defiant.

"She used to say, *'Langston, never beg to enter rooms that your spirit already outshines.'* And yet, here we are. Still fighting for entry into places we built."

Memory Insert – 1969, Harlem New York

Patty Crocker sat in a folding chair in her small living room, plastic still covering the sofa, a cup of instant coffee balanced on the armrest. Nelson Langford had stopped by, bringing her a copy of *The Philadelphian*.

He placed it on her coffee table. "This one's not for you to read, Patty. It's for the boy. One day, he'll understand what this world does to men who try to walk through gilded doors without a golden name."

Patty looked at the cover but didn't open it. "If it'll help Langston, I'll keep it safe." She tucked the book beside the family Bible.

Back to Present – ScholarForge Seminar

Langston stood in front of a projection screen. One side displayed a slide of *The Philadelphian*'s cover: the other, Du Bois's *The Souls of Black Folk*.

He addressed the room.

"Today's question: Is assimilation a form of resistance—or erasure?"

Marcus stood, eyes steady. "Powell's protagonist becomes the top of his field, but he's constantly reminded that status doesn't equal acceptance. He challenges them in the courtroom, but socially, they never let him in."

Langston added, "Baruch gave advice from a bench. Powell's character challenged the bench itself. And Du Bois? He gave us the framework to understand the double consciousness behind it all."

Another student raised their hand. "So, what's the solution? Play their game or rewrite the rules?"

Langston looked out over the room. "The answer isn't either/or. It's *memory and mission*. If you must enter the house, do so knowing where your blueprint lies. If you build your own—don't imitate their chandeliers. Illuminate with your truth."

That night, in the silence of his study, Langston returned *The Philadelphian* to its rightful place—between *The Crisis* and *The Miseducation of the Negro*.

Tucked inside was a fresh sheet of paper from Marcus. It read:

"They don't have to say it. They just look at you in a certain way, and you know." — *The Philadelphian*

Langston smiled softly.

"Let the new architects rise—with the right blueprint in hand."

Epilogue: The Curriculum We Carry

The forge never closes. It adapts. Some teach with slides. Others teach with scars. But the students—those whose names are rarely carved into the monuments—carry the curriculum now. In barbershop libraries. In coding bootcamps in church basements. In whispered bedtime stories layered with strategy. ScholarForge wasn't about one man. It was about the moment a community remembered its power.
Langston's last journal entry read simply: "Teach like the storm is already here. Love like the future is already watching."
Because it is.
And it's waiting to be taught.

Later that evening, as the sun dipped low over the trees behind Graham Manor, Marcus was called into the study.
Langston stood at the desk—his posture relaxed, but his eyes sharp as ever. He gestured toward a black box trimmed in brass.

"Open it," he said quietly.

Inside was a Moroccan leather journal, deep oxblood, still crisp but not untouched. Embossed in the center was the ScholarForge crest: an anvil atop a scroll, flanked by two feathers. The motto beneath it gleamed in gold leaf— *"Memory Is Resistance."* Marcus looked up.

Langston gave the faintest smile. "Every generation earns the right to write its own entries. That one's yours."

Marcus opened it gently. The pages were blank—waiting. But inside the front cover was a single line, written in Langston's hand:

"What we do is not to be remembered. What we do is to remember." —L.E.G.

"I don't know what to write," Marcus admitted, still holding the book like something sacred.

"You will," Langston said. "And when the time comes—don't write what's safe. Write what they tried to erase."

They stood there in quiet agreement, two scholars in different stages of the same fight.

Outside, the wind shifted, and somewhere
in the distance, a church bell rang.

Vignette: The Price Paid Twice

Atlas Club, Private Salon   The fire crackled low in the private salon of the Atlas Club, its quiet hum barely audible above the warm murmur of post dinner conversation.
Langston Graham sat in a corner alcove, surrounded by books, glass, and history. Judge Hamilton Cole sat across from him, retired but still sharp, a man whose voice once thundered in federal courtrooms but now moved with measured restraint. Between them, a bottle of Elijah Craig 18year bourbon rested beside two glasses.
"Langston," the judge said, "I keep hearing you say that student debt was 'by design.' I don't know if I buy that." He paused, then added with quiet pride, "I paid mine. So did my daughter. We didn't ask for relief. We handled ours." Langston set his cigar gently in the ashtray, then folded his hands—gold signet ring glinting in the firelight. "You did," he said, nodding with respect. "And I honor that. What you did took discipline, grit, and

grace. But surviving a rigged system doesn't make that system just. It only proves how extraordinary you were to make it through." The judge raised an eyebrow but didn't interrupt.

Langston leaned in, voice calm, deliberate. "You paid off your debt. That's the headline. But the footnote? Years of delayed ownership. Family dreams postponed. Entire careers built around loan repayment instead of passion. You didn't just pay in dollars—you paid in time, in peace, in opportunity."

"That," he said, "was by design." "The system didn't set you up to thrive. It set you up to comply. To believe that struggle was proof of worth. That bondage was noble if you wore it quietly." "You escaped the trap. But the trap is still there."

The judge's hand tightened slightly around his glass.

Langston continued.

"Some people hear debt forgiveness and think it's about being fair to those who didn't pay. But the real injustice? Is letting it continue at all. If we know the bridge is burning, why are we charging tolls to cross it?"

He poured two fingers of bourbon into the judge's glass.

"This isn't about you. It's about what comes after you. We honor what you endured—but we break the system, so your granddaughter doesn't have to." He handed over the glass and lifted his own. "To the ones who paid." A clink.

"And to those who never should've had to."
The fire popped once, like punctuation.
Neither man spoke for a long while. But both sat a little straighter.

Author's Note on Sources

This is a work of fiction grounded in fact.
Throughout *The Graham Files: Shattered
Mandates*, real historical figures, events,
and quotations are woven into the
narrative to reflect enduring struggles over
education, justice, memory, and belonging.
Every direct quote attributed to historical
figures—such as Bernard Baruch, W.E.B.
Du Bois, Howard Thurman, and others—
has been carefully verified. Likewise,
references to books, legislation, and
political history are based on documented
sources.

This novel stands in a tradition that values
the intersection of truth and imagination—
using story not to escape history, but to
interrogate it.

The following is a selection of key texts
quoted or referenced in the novel. Readers
are encouraged to explore these works
further to deepen their understanding of
the legacy these characters carry forward.

Selected Bibliography

Baruch, Bernard M.
Baruch: My Own Story. New York: Holt,
Rinehart and Winston, 1957.

Clarke, John Henrik.
*John Henrik Clarke: A Great and Mighty
Walk.* Directed by St. Clair Bourne, 1996.

Crummell, Alexander.
*The Future of Africa: Being Addresses,
Sermons, Etc., Delivered in the Republic of
Liberia.* New York: Negro Universities
Press, 1862.

Douglass, Frederick.
Selected Speeches and Writings. Edited by
Philip S. Foner. Chicago: Lawrence Hill
Books, 1999.

Du Bois, W.E.B.
The Souls of Black Folk. Chicago: A.C.
McClurg & Co., 1903.

Gates, Henry Louis, Jr. *Stony the
Road: Reconstruction, White
Supremacy, and the Rise of Jim Crow.*
New York: Penguin Press, 2019.

Grimké, Francis J.
*The Negro: His Rights and Wrongs, the
Forces for Him and Against Him.*
Washington, D.C.: W.H. Roberts, 1898.

Mays, Benjamin E.
Born to Rebel: An Autobiography. Athens:
University of Georgia Press, 1987.

Powell, Richard.
The Philadelphian. New York: Charles Scribner's Sons, 1956.

Proctor, Samuel DeWitt. *My Moral Odyssey.* Valley Forge: Judson Press, 1989.

Thurman, Howard.
Jesus and the Disinherited. Boston: Beacon Press, 1949.

Washington, Booker T. *Up from Slavery.* New York: Doubleday, Page & Co., 1901.

Woodson, Carter G.
The Miseducation of the Negro. Washington, D.C.: Associated Publishers, 1933.

The Crisis Magazine. Published by the NAACP, founded by W.E.B. Du Bois in 1910.